The skin of her palm was
warm. He found himself wondering
what it would feel like to have her
massage the aching tension out of
his neck.

Matt pulled his hand away, as if to tug himself
away from where his thoughts were wandering.
It had been so long since he'd felt a woman's
touch. For six long, lonely years he had ignored
the natural stirrings of his body, distracting himself
with work until there wasn't time or energy to think
about what he was missing.

No one in all that time had made his skin lift and
tighten simultaneously at the merest touch. No
one's eyes had met his and seen more than he had
wanted them to see. No one's smile had melted or
even chipped at the stone of sadness that weighed
down his soul.

But Dr. Kellie Thorne, with her featherlight touch,
caramel-brown eyes and beautiful smile, certainly
came close.

Perhaps a little too close.

Dear Reader,

As a writer I am constantly on the search for inspiration, but often things happen without me even realizing I could use it in a book.

The idea for this story started when my surgeon husband and I flew to Roma in Outback Queensland where he was to conduct a trauma course for regional doctors. I met so many lovely dedicated doctors and nurses there!

The isolation of Outback areas is always a stark reminder of what we take for granted in the city—including potential brides and bridegrooms! I decided to send my heroine Kellie Thorne out to Culwulla Creek for reasons other than to find a husband, but when she meets Matt McNaught the sparks fly instantly. He is brooding and surly, and she is bubbly and bouncing full of energy.

I love working with characters who are polar opposites because, while on the surface they appear to have nothing in common, deeper down they truly complement each other. Matt has suffered a heart-wrenching loss, and it is only when Kellie bounds into town that he is forced to put the past where it belongs—well and truly behind him.

While you read this story, spare a thought for the dedicated medical personnel, police, pilots and ground crew who bring medical help to those who need it wherever they may be in the big wide beautiful world of the Australian Outback.

Best wishes,

Melanie Milburne

TOP-NOTCH DOC, OUTBACK BRIDE
Melanie Milburne

HARLEQUIN®

TORONTO • NEW YORK • LONDON
AMSTERDAM • PARIS • SYDNEY • HAMBURG
STOCKHOLM • ATHENS • TOKYO • MILAN • MADRID
PRAGUE • WARSAW • BUDAPEST • AUCKLAND

Recycling programs
for this product may
not exist in your area.

ISBN-13: 978-0-373-06709-1

TOP-NOTCH DOC, OUTBACK BRIDE

First North American Publication 2009

Copyright © 2009 by Melanie Milburne

www.eHarlequin.com

Printed in U.S.A.

TOP-NOTCH DOC, OUTBACK BRIDE

To my dear friend and confidante
Fiona Abercrombie-Howroyd. You never fail
to amaze me with how you take life on with both
hands, and when someone raises the bar you don't
balk but leap right over it. I am so proud of you
and both of your gorgeous boys.

CHAPTER ONE

IT WASN'T the worst flight Kellie had ever been on but it certainly came pretty close. The three-hour delay at Brisbane airport had been annoying enough, but when she had finally boarded the twenty-seat regional service area plane she found a man was already sitting in *her* window seat.

'Er…excuse me,' she said, holding her boarding pass up. 'I think you are in the wrong seat. *I* am 10A, you must be 10B.'

The man looked up from the thick black book he was reading. 'Would you like me to move?' he asked in a tone that seemed to suggest he thought it would be totally unreasonable of her to expect him to unfold his long length from the cramped space he was currently jammed into.

Something about the slightly arrogant set to his features made Kellie respond tartly, 'I do, actually, yes. I always have a window seat. I specifically ask for it each time. I feel claustrophobic if I can't see outside.'

Using his boarding pass as a bookmark, the man got to his feet and squeezed out of the two-seat row, his tall figure towering over Kellie as he brushed past her to allow her room to get in.

She felt the warmth of his body and her nostrils began to flare slightly as she tried to place his aftershave. Living with six men had made her a bit of an expert on male colognes, but this time she couldn't decide if the primary citrus scent was lime or lemon based.

She gave him a cool little smile and wriggled past him to sit down, but just as he was about to resume his seat she realised she didn't have enough space under the seat in front for her handbag as well as her hand luggage. 'Um…' she said, swivelling back around to face him. 'Would you mind putting this in the overhead locker for me?'

He *did* mind, Kellie could tell. He didn't say a word but his impossibly dark blue eyes gave a small but still detectable roll of irritation as he took her bag and placed it in the compartment above.

He sat back down beside her and, methodically clipping his belt into place, returned to his book, his left arm resting on *her* armrest.

Kellie inwardly fumed. It happened just about every time she flew and it was *always* a man, although she couldn't help noticing that this one was a great improvement on any of the passengers she'd been seated next to in the past. He even smelt a whole lot better too, she decided as she caught another faint but alluring whiff of lemon-lime as she leaned down to stuff her handbag underneath the seat in front.

While she was down there she noticed he was wearing elastic-sided boots. They weren't dusty or particularly scuffed, which probably meant he was a cattle farmer who had dressed in his best to fly down to the big smoke on business and was now returning home. His long legs were encased in moleskin trousers and the sleeves of his light blue cotton shirt were rolled halfway up his lean but strong-looking and deeply tanned forearms.

Yep, definitely a farmer, Kellie decided, although she couldn't see any sign of him having recently worn a hat.

Didn't all Queensland cattle farmers wear hats? she mused. She noted his dark brown hair wasn't crumpled but neatly styled, so neatly styled, in fact, she could make out the tiny grooves from a recent comb that had passed through the thick wavy strands.

She sat back in her seat and for the sake of common politeness forced herself to give him a friendly smile. 'Thank you for moving. I really appreciate it.'

His dark eyes met hers and assessed her for a moment before he grunted, 'It's fine,' before his head went back to the book he was holding.

Right, then, Kellie thought sourly as she searched for both ends of her seat belt. *Don't make polite conversation with me, then. See if I care.*

She gave the left hand belt end a little tug but it wouldn't budge from where it was lodged. 'Er…excuse me,' she said with a frosty look his way. 'You're sitting on my seat belt.'

The man turned to look at her again, his tanned forehead frowning slightly. 'I'm sorry, did you say something?' he asked.

Kellie pointed to the unclipped device in her hand. 'I need the other end of this and, rather than go digging for it myself, I thought it would be polite to ask you to remove it yourself,' she said with a pert tilt of her chin.

Another faint flicker of annoyance came and went in his gaze as he removed the buckle and strap from the back of his seat and handed it to her silently.

'Thank you,' she said, her fingers brushing against his in spite of her effort to avoid doing so. She gave her fingers a quick on-off clench to remove the tingling sensation the brief touch had caused, but still it lingered under the surface of her skin as if he had sent an electric charge right through her body.

That he wasn't similarly affected couldn't have been more

obvious. He simply returned to his book, turning the next page and reading on with unwavering concentration, and even though the flight attendant asked for everyone's attention while she went through the mandatory safety procedure, he remained engrossed in whatever he was reading.

Typical thinks-he-knows-it-all male, Kellie thought as she made a point of leaning forward with a totally absorbed expression on her face as the flight attendant rattled off her spiel, even though Kellie knew she herself was probably better qualified if an emergency were to occur given what had happened two years ago on another regional flight.

But, then, after four years in a busy GP practice she felt she had enough experience to handle most emergencies, although she had to admit her confidence would be little on the dented side without her well-equipped doctor's bag at hand. But at least it was safely packed in the baggage hold along with her four cases to tide her over for the six-month locum in the Queensland outback, she reassured herself.

Once the flight attendant had instructed everyone to sit back and enjoy the one-and-a-half-hour flight to Culwulla Creek, Kellie took a couple of deep calming breaths as the plane began to head for the runway, the throb and choking roar of the engines doing nothing to allay her fears. She scrunched her eyes closed and in the absence of an available armrest clasped her hands in her lap.

You can do this. She ran through her usual pep talk. You've flown hundreds of times, even across time zones. You know the statistics: you have more chance of being killed on the way to and from the airport than during the actual flight. One little engine failure in the past doesn't mean it's going to happen again. Lightning doesn't strike in the same place twice, right?

The plane rattled and rumbled down the runway, faster and

faster, until finally putting its nose in the air and taking off, the heavy clunk of landing gear returning to its compartment making Kellie's eyes suddenly spring open. 'That was the landing gear, right?' she asked the silent figure beside her. 'Please, tell me that was the landing gear and not something else.'

The bluer-than-blue eyes stared unblinkingly at her for a moment before he answered. 'Yes,' he said, but this time his tone contained more than a hint of sarcasm. 'That was the landing gear. All planes have it, even ones as small as this.'

'I knew *that*,' Kellie said huffily. 'It's just it sounded as if…you know…something wasn't quite right.'

'If everything wasn't quite right, we would have turned back by now,' he pointed out in an I-am-so-bored-with-this-conversation tone as he returned his attention to his book.

Kellie glanced surreptitiously at the book to see if she recognised the title but it wasn't one she was familiar with. It had a boring sort of cover in any case, which probably meant he was a boring sort of person. Although he was a very good-looking boring person, she had to admit as she sneaked another little glance at his profile. He was in his early thirties, thirty-two or -three, she thought, and had a cleanly shaven chiselled jaw and a long straight nose. His lips were well shaped, but she couldn't help thinking they looked as if they rarely made the effort to stretch into a smile.

Her gaze slipped to his hands where he was holding his book. He had long fingers, dusted with dark hair, and his nails were short but clean, which she found a little unusual for a cattle farmer. Didn't they always have dust or cattle feed or farm machinery grease embedded around their cuticles? But perhaps he had been away for a week or two, enjoying the comforts of a city hotel, she thought.

Kellie shifted restlessly in her seat as the plane gained

altitude, wondering how long it would be before the seat-belt sign went off so she could visit the lavatory. She mentally crossed her legs and looked down at her handbag wedged under the seat. She considered retrieving the magazine she had bought to read but just then the flight attendant announced that the captain had turned off the seat-belt sign so it was now safe to move about the cabin.

Kellie unclipped her belt and got to her feet. 'Excuse me,' she said with a sheepish look at the man sitting beside her. 'I have to go to the toilet.'

His gaze collided with hers for another brief moment before he closed the book with exaggerated precision, unclipped his seat belt, unfolded himself from the seat and stood to one side, his expression now blank, although Kellie could again sense his irritation. She could feel it pushing against her, the invisible pressure making her want to shrink away from his presence.

She squeezed past him, sucking in her stomach and her chest in case she touched him inadvertently. 'Thank you,' she said, feeling her face beginning to redden. 'I'll try not to be too long.'

'Take all the time you need,' he said with a touch of dryness.

Kellie set her mouth and moved down the aisle, her back straight with pride, even though her face was feeling hot all over again. *Get a grip*, she told herself sternly. Don't let him intimidate you. No doubt you'll meet thousands…well, hundreds at least…of men just like him in the bush. Besides, wasn't she some sort of expert on men?

Well…apart from that brief and utterly painful and totally embarrassing and ego-crushing episode with Harley Edwards—yes, she was.

When Kellie came back to her seat a few minutes later she felt more than a little relieved to find her co-passenger's seat empty. She scanned the rest of the passenger rows to see if he had changed seats, but he was up at the front of the plane, bending down to talk to someone on the right-hand aisle.

Kellie sat back down and looked out of the window, the shimmering heat haze of the drought-stricken outback making her think a little longingly of the bustling-with-activity beach-side home in Newcastle in NSW she had left behind, not to mention her father and five younger brothers.

But it was well and truly time to move on; they needed to learn to stand on their own twelve feet, Kellie reminded herself. It was what her mother would have wanted her to do, to follow her own path, not to try and take up the achingly empty space her mother's death had left behind six years ago.

The man returned to his seat just as the refreshment trolley made its way up the aisle. He barely glanced at her as he sat back down, but his elbow brushed against hers as he tried to commandeer the armrest.

Kellie gave him a sugar-sweet smile and kept her arm where it was. 'You have one on the other side,' she said.

The space between his dark brows narrowed slightly. 'What?'

She pointed to the armrest on his right. 'You have another armrest over there,' she said.

There was a tight little silence.

'So do you.' He nodded towards the vacant armrest against the window.

'Yes, but I don't see why you get to have the choice of two,' she returned. 'Isn't that rather selfish of you to automatically assume every available armrest is yours?'

'I am not assuming anything,' he said in a clipped tone, and, shifting his gaze from hers, reached for his book in the seat pocket, opened it and added, 'If you want the armrest, have it. It makes no difference to me.'

Kellie watched him out of the corner of her eye as he read the next nine pages of his book. He was a very fast reader and the print was rather small, which impressed her considering how for years she'd had to bribe and threaten and cajole each of her brothers into reading anything besides the back of the cereal packet each morning.

The flight attendant approached and, smiling at Kellie, asked, 'Would you like to purchase a drink or snack from the trolley this afternoon?'

Kellie smiled back as she undid the fold-down table. 'I would love a diet cola with ice and lemon if you have it.'

The flight attendant handed her the plastic cup half-filled with ice and a tiny sliver of lemon before passing over the opened can of soda. 'That will be three dollars,' she said.

Kellie bit her lip. Her bag was stuffed as far under the seat in front as she could get it and, with the tray table down, retrieving it was going to take the sort of flexibility no one but Houdini possessed. 'Er…would you mind holding these for me while I get my purse from my bag?' she asked.

He took the cup and can with a little roll-like flutter of his eyelids but didn't say a word.

Kellie rummaged in her bag for her purse and finally found the right change but in passing it over to the flight attendant somehow knocked the opened can of cola out of the man's hand and straight into his lap.

'What the—' He bit back the rough expletive that had come to his lips and glared at her as he got to his feet, the dark bubbles of liquid soaking through his moleskins like a pool of blood.

'Oops…' Kellie said a little lamely.

'I'll get some paper towels for you, Dr McNaught,' the flight attendant said, and rushed away.

Kellie sat in gob-smacked silence as the name filtered through her brain.

Dr McNaught?

She swallowed to get her heart to return to its rightful place in her chest. It couldn't be…could it?

Dr Matthew McNaught?

She blinked and looked up at him, wincing slightly as she encountered his diamond-hard dark blue glare. '*You're* Dr Matthew McNaught?' she asked, 'from the two-GP practice in Culwulla Creek?'

'Yes,' he said, his lips pulled tight. 'Let me guess,' he added with a distinct curl of his top lip. 'You're the new locum, right?'

Kellie felt herself sink even further into the limited space available. 'Y-yes,' she squeaked. 'How did you guess?'

CHAPTER TWO

THE flight attendant came bustling back just then with a thick wad of paper towels and Kellie watched helplessly as Dr McNaught mopped up what he could of the damage.

'I hope it doesn't stain,' Kellie said, trying not to stare too long at his groin. 'I'll pay for dry-cleaning costs of course.'

'That won't be necessary,' he said. 'Besides, there's no dry cleaner in Culwulla Creek. There's not even a laundromat.'

'Oh…' Kellie said, wondering not for the first time what she had flung herself into by agreeing to this post. 'I'm not usually so clumsy. I have a very steady hand normally.'

He gave her a sweeping glance before he resumed his seat. 'You're going to need it out here,' he said. 'The practice serves an area covering several hundred square kilometres. The nearest hospital is in Roma but all the emergency or acute cases have to be flown to Brisbane. It's not going to be a walk in the park, I can tell you.'

'I never for a moment thought it would be,' Kellie said, a little miffed that he obviously thought her a city girl with no practical skills. 'I'm used to hard work.'

'Have you worked in a remote outback area before?' he asked.

Kellie hesitated over her answer. She was thinking her six-week stint in Tamworth in northern New South Wales

probably wouldn't qualify. It was a regional area, not exactly the outback. 'Um…not really,' she said. 'But I'm keen to learn the ropes.'

His eyes studied her for a moment. 'What made you decide to take this post?' he asked.

'I liked the sound of working in the bush,' she answered. *And I desperately needed to get away from my family and my absolutely disastrous love life*, she mentally tacked on. 'And six months will just fly by, I imagine.'

'It's not everyone's cup of tea,' he said. 'The hours are long and the cases sometimes difficult to manage, with the issues of distance and limited resources.'

'So who is holding the fort right now?' she asked.

'There's a semi-retired GP, David Cutler, who fills in occasionally,' he said. 'He runs a clinic once a month to keep up his skills but his health isn't good. His wife, Trish, is the practice receptionist and we have one nurse, Rosie Duncan. We could do with more but that's the way it is out here.'

Kellie let a little silence slip past before she asked. 'How long have you been at Culwulla Creek?'

His gaze remained focused on the book in the seat pocket in front of him. 'Six years,' he answered.

'Wow, you must really love it out here,' she said.

He hesitated for a mere sliver of a second before he answered, 'Yes.'

Kellie watched as his expression closed off like a pair of curtains being pulled across a window. She had seen that look before, far too many times, in fact, on the faces of her father and brothers whenever she happened to nudge in under their emotional radar. It was a male thing. They liked to keep some things private and somehow she suspected Dr Matthew McNaught, too, had quite a few no-go areas.

'By the way, I'm Kellie Thorne,' she said offering him her hand.

His hand was cool and firm as it briefly took hers. 'Matthew McNaught, but Matt's fine.'

'Matt, then,' she said, smiling.

He didn't return her smile.

'So…' She rolled her lips together and began again. 'Do you have a family out here with you? A wife and kids perhaps?'

'No.'

Kellie was starting to see why he hadn't been successful thus far in landing himself a life partner. In spite of his good looks he had no personality to speak of. She felt like a tennis-ball throwing machine—she kept sending conversation starters his way but he didn't make any effort to return them.

Not only that, he hadn't once looked at her with anything remotely resembling male interest. Kellie knew she was being stupidly insecure thanks to her disastrous relationship—if you could call it that—with Harley Edwards, but surely Matt McNaught could have at least done a double-take, like the young pilot had on the tarmac before they had boarded the plane.

Kellie had looked in enough mirrors in her time to know none of them were in any danger of breaking any time soon. She had her mother's slim but still femininely curvy figure and her chestnut brown hair was mid-length, with just a hint of a wave running through it. Her toffee-brown eyes had thick sooty lashes, which saved her a fortune in mascara. Her teeth were white and straight thanks to two and a half years of torture wearing braces when she'd been in her teens, and her skin was clear and naturally sun-kissed from spending so much time with her brothers at the beach.

Maybe he was gay, she pondered as she watched him read another chapter of his book. That would account for the zero

interest. Anyway, she wasn't out here on the hunt for a love life, far from it. So what if her one and only lover had bludgeoned her self-esteem? She didn't need to find a replacement just to prove he was a two-timing sleazeball jerk with…

OK. That's enough, Kellie chided herself as she wriggled again to get comfortable. Get over it. Harley probably hasn't given you another thought since that morning you arrived to find him in bed with his secretary. Kellie winced at the memory and looked out of the window again, letting out the tiniest of sighs.

This locum position couldn't have come at a better time and the short time was perfect. Living in the outback for a lengthy time was definitely not her thing. She would see the six months out but no longer. She had been a beach chick from birth. She had more bikinis than most women had shoes. Not only that, she was a fully qualified lifesaver, the sound of the ocean like a pulse in her blood. This would be the longest period she had been away from the coast but it would be worth it if it achieved what she hoped it would achieve.

The seat-belt light suddenly came on and the captain announced that there might be some stronger than normal turbulence ahead.

Kellie turned to Matthew with wide eyes. 'Do you think we'll be all right?' she asked.

He looked at her as if she had grown a third eye. 'You *have* flown before, haven't you?' he asked.

'Yes, but not usually in something this small,' she confessed.

He let out a sound, something between derision and incredulity. 'You do realise you will be flying in a Beechcraft twin engine plane at least once if not three or four times a month, don't you? It's called the Royal Flying Doctor Service and out here lives depend on it.'

Kellie gave a gulping swallow as the plane gave a stomach-dropping lurch. 'I know, but someone will have to stay at the practice surely? Tim Montgomery said it in one of the letters he sent,' she said. Biting her lip, she added, 'I was kind of hoping that could be me.'

His eyes gave a little roll. 'I knew this was going to happen,' he muttered.

'What?' she asked, wincing as the plane shifted again.

His blue eyes clashed momentarily with hers. 'This is no doubt Tim and his wife Claire's doing,' he said. 'I asked for someone with plenty of outback experience and instead what do I get?'

'You get me,' Kellie said with a hitch of her chin. 'I've been in practice for four years and I'm EMST trained.'

'And you have a fear of flying.' He settled his shoulders back against the seat. 'Great.'

Kellie gritted her teeth. 'I do *not* have a fear of flying. I've been on heaps of flights. I even went to New Zealand last year.'

She could tell he wasn't impressed. He gave her another rolled-eye look and turned back to his book.

'What are you reading?' she asked, after the turbulence had faded and the seat-belt light had been turned off again. Talking was good. It helped to keep her calm. It helped her not to notice all those suspicious mechanical noises.

'It's a book on astronomy,' he said without looking up from the pages.

'Is it any good?'

Matt let out a frustrated sigh and turned to look at her. 'Yes, it is,' he said. 'Would you like to borrow it?' *Anything to shut you up*, he thought. What was it with this young woman? Didn't she see he was in no mood for idle conversation? And what the hell was she doing, arriving a week earlier than expected?

She shook her head. 'Nope, I don't do heavy stuff any more. The only things I read now are medical journals and magazines and the occasional light novel.'

'I'm doing a degree in astronomy online through Swinburne University,' Matt said, hoping she would take the hint and let him get on with his chapter on globular clusters. 'There's a lot of reading, and I have an exam coming up.'

'You're a very fast reader,' she said. 'Have you done a speed-reading course or something?'

Matt's eyes were starting to feel strained from the repeated rolling. 'No, it's just that I enjoy reading,' he said. 'It fills in the time.'

'So it's pretty quiet out here, huh?' she asked.

Matt looked at her again, *really* looked at her this time. She had a pretty heart-shaped face and her eyes were an unusual caramel brown. He couldn't quite decide how long her hair was as she had it sort of twisted up in a haphazard ponytail-cum-knot at the back of her head, but it was glossy and thick and there was plenty of it, and every now and again he caught of whiff of the honeysuckle fragrance of her shampoo.

She had a nice figure, trim and toned and yet feminine in all the right places. Her mouth was a little on the pouting side, he'd noticed earlier, but when she smiled it reminded him of a ray of bright sunshine breaking through dark clouds.

'No, it's not exactly quiet,' he answered. 'It's different, that's all.'

She gave him another little smile. 'So no nightclubs and five-star restaurants, right?'

Matt felt a familiar tight ache deep inside his chest and looked away. 'No,' he said. 'No nightclubs, no cinemas, no fine dining, no twenty-four-hour trading.' *And no Madeleine*, he added silently.

'What about taxis?' she asked after a short pause. 'Do you have any of those?'

His eyes came back to hers. 'No, but I can give you a lift to Tim and Claire's house. I take it that's where you're staying?'

She nodded. 'It was so kind of them to offer their house and the use of their car while I'm here. They sent me the keys in the mail. Believe me, that would never happen in the city. People don't lend you anything, especially virtual strangers.'

Matt wondered again what had attracted her to the post. He even wondered if Tim and Claire and Trish had colluded to make the job as attractive as possible in order to secure a female GP, a young and single female GP at that—or so he assumed from her ring-free fingers.

'So what do people do out here in their spare time?' she asked. 'Apart from reading, of course.'

'Most of the locals are on the land,' he said. 'They have plenty to do to keep them occupied, especially with this drought going on and on.'

'That's what I thought you were at first,' she said. 'I had you pegged as a cattle farmer.'

'I've actually got a few hectares of my own,' he said, doing his best to ignore the brilliance of her smile. 'I bought them a couple of years back off an elderly farmer who needed to sell in a hurry. I've got some breeding stock I'm trying to keep going until we get some decent rain.'

'Is that where you live?'

'Yes, it's only a few minutes out of town.'

'So do you have horses and stuff?' she asked.

Matt looked longingly at his book. 'Yeah, a couple, but they're pretty wild.'

'I love horses,' she said, snuggling into her seat again. 'I used to ride a bit as a child.'

The captain announced that they were preparing to land and she looked out of the window at the barren landscape. 'So where's the creek?' she asked, and, turning back to him, continued, 'I mean, there has to be a creek somewhere. Culwulla Creek must be named after a creek, right?'

Matt only just managed to control the urge to roll his eyes heavenwards yet again. 'Yes, there is, but it's practically dry. There's been barely a trickle of water for more than three years.'

Her face fell a little. 'Oh…that's a shame.'

'Why is that?' he found himself asking, even though he really didn't want to know.

'I live by the beach,' she said. 'I swim every day, rain or shine.'

Matt felt his chest tighten again. Madeleine had loved swimming. 'That's one hobby you'll have to suspend while you're out here,' he said in a flat, emotionless tone. 'That is, unless it rains.'

'Oh, well, then,' she said with a bright optimistic smile. 'I'd better start doing a rain dance or something. Who knows what might happen?'

Who indeed, Matt thought as the plane descended to land.

Kellie unclipped her seat belt once the plane had landed and reached for her handbag. Matt had risen to retrieve her bulging cabin bag from the overhead locker and silently handed it to her before he took out his own small overnight travel case.

'So how far is it to town?' she asked as they walked across the blistering heat of the tarmac as few minutes later.

'Ten minutes.'

'Tim and Claire's house is a couple of streets away from the practice, isn't it?' she asked as they waited for her luggage to be unloaded.

'Yes.'

She waved away a fly. 'Gosh, it's awfully hot, isn't it?'

'Yes.'

Right, Kellie thought, that's it. I'm not even going to try and make conversation. She'd spent the last six years with a house full of monosyllabic males—the last thing she needed was another one in her life.

She looked up to see an older woman in her mid-fifties coming towards them. 'How did the weekend go, Matt?' she asked in a gentle, concerned voice.

Kellie watched as Matt moved his lips into a semblance of a smile but it was gone before it had time to settle long enough to transform his features.

'It was OK,' he said. 'John and Mary-Anne were very welcoming as usual, but you know how it is.'

The older woman grimaced in empathy. 'It's tough on everyone. Birthdays are the worst.'

'Yeah,' he said with another attempt at a smile. 'They are.'

Kellie was intrigued with the little exchange but before she had time to speculate any further, the older woman glanced past Matt's broad shoulder and smiled. 'Well, hello there,' she said. 'Welcome to Culwulla Creek. Are you a tourist or visiting a friend?'

'I'm the new locum filling in for Tim Montgomery,' Kellie said, extending her hand. 'I'm Kellie Thorne.'

'Oh, my goodness, aren't you gorgeous?' the woman gushed as she grasped both of Kellie's hands in her soft motherly ones. 'I had no idea they had someone so young and attractive in mind.'

Kellie felt her face go hot but it had nothing to do with the furnace-like temperature of the October afternoon. She smiled self-consciously as she felt the press of Matt

McNaught's gaze as if he was assessing her physical attributes for the first time.

'I'm Ruth Williams,' the older woman said. 'It's wonderful you could come to fill in for Tim while he and Claire are overseas. So tell me, where are you from?'

'Newcastle, in NSW. I did my medical training and internship there as well,' Kellie answered.

Ruth smiled with genuine warmth. 'What a thrill to have you here. We've never had a female GP before, have we, Matt?'

'No,' Matt said, frowning when he saw the luggage trailer lumbering towards them. In amongst the usual assortment of black and brown and battered bags with a few tattered ribbons attached to various handles to make identification easier, there were four hot pink suitcases, each of which looked as if their fastenings were being stretched to the limit.

Kellie followed the line of his gaze and mentally grimaced. Maybe she had overdone it on the packing thing, she thought. But how was a girl to survive six months in the bush without all the feminine accoutrements?

'I take it these are yours?' Matt asked, as he nodded towards the trailer.

She captured her bottom lip for a second. 'I have a problem travelling lightly. I've been working on it but I guess I'm not quite there, huh?'

He didn't roll his eyes but he came pretty close, Kellie thought but she also thought, she saw his lips twitch slightly, which for some inexplicable reason secretly delighted her.

'It's all right, Dr Thorne,' Ruth piped up. 'Dr McNaught has a four-wheel-drive vehicle so it will all fit in.'

'Er…great,' Kellie said, watching fixatedly as Matt's biceps bulged as he lifted each case off the trailer.

'I'm afraid there are no basic foodstuffs at Tim and Claire's house,' Ruth said with a worried pleat of her brow. 'I would have bought you some milk and bread but we thought you were coming next week so I didn't organise anything, and the corner store will be closed by now.'

'It's all right,' Kellie assured her. 'I had lots of nibbles in the members' lounge while I waited for the flight to be called and I've got some chocolate in one of my bags. My brothers gave it to me. That will tide me over.'

'That was sweet of them,' Ruth said. 'How many brothers do you have?'

'I have five,' Kellie answered, 'all younger than me.'

Ruth's eyes bulged. '*Five?* Oh, dear, your poor mother. How on earth does she cope?'

Kellie concentrated on securing her handbag over her shoulder as she reached for one of the pink suitcases. 'She died six years ago,' she said, stripping her voice of the raw emotion she—in spite of all her efforts—still occasionally felt. 'That's why I took this outback post.' *Or, at least, one of the reasons*, she thought. 'My father and brothers have become a bit too dependent on me,' she said. 'I think they need to learn to take more responsibility for themselves. It's well and truly time to move on, don't you think?'

Matt still wore a blank expression but Ruth touched Kellie on the arm and gave it a gentle comforting squeeze, her warm brown eyes misting slightly. 'Not everyone moves on at the same pace, my dear, but it's wise that you're giving them the opportunity,' she said. 'It's very brave of you to come so far from home. I hope it works out for you and for them.'

'Thank you,' Kellie said, glancing at the tall, silent figure standing nearby, his expression still shuttered. 'I hope so, too.'

CHAPTER THREE

IT WAS quite a juggling act, getting the whole of Kellie's luggage into the back of Matt's vehicle, even though he had only his carry-on bag with him. But there were other things in the rear of his car—tow ropes, a spare tyre and what looked to be his doctor's bag, as it was very similar to hers, and a big box of mechanical tools, as well as a few pieces of hay scattered about.

Kellie stood to one side as he jostled everything into position and once the hatchback was closed she moved to the passenger side, but before she could open the door he had got there first and opened it for her.

'Thanks,' she said, feeling a little taken aback by his courteous gesture. Over the years she had become so used to her brothers diving into the family people-mover, each vying for the best seat with little regard for her comfort, that his gallantry took her completely by surprise.

'Mrs Williams seems like a lovely lady,' she said as she caught sight of the older woman driving off ahead of them to the road leading to town. 'Did she come out to the airport just to see you? She doesn't appear to have picked anyone up.'

'Ruth Williams comes out to meet every flight,' Matt said as he shifted the gears. 'She's been doing it for years.'

'Why is that?' Kellie asked, turning to look at him.

His gaze never wavered from the road ahead. 'Her teenage daughter disappeared twenty years ago. Ruth has never quite given up hope that one day Tegan will get off one of the thrice-weekly flights, so she meets each one just in case.'

Kellie frowned. 'How terribly sad. Did her daughter run away or was it likely to have been something more sinister?'

His dark blue eyes met hers for a moment before returning to the long straight stretch of road ahead. 'She went missing without trace,' he said. 'As far as I know, the case is still open.'

'Did she go missing from here?' she asked.

'Yes,' he answered. 'She was fourteen, nearly fifteen years old. She caught the bus home from school, she was seen walking along the main street at around four-thirty and then she disappeared. No one has seen or heard from her since. The police lost valuable time thinking it was just another bored country kid running away from home. Tegan had run away a couple of times before. Ruth's now late husband, Tegan's step-father, apparently wasn't the easiest man to live with. It was understandable that they assumed the girl had hitched a ride out of town. She was a bit of a rebel around these parts, truanting, shoplifting, driving without a licence, that sort of thing.'

'But no one's ever found out what happened to her?' Kellie asked with a frown.

He shook his head. 'There was no sign of a struggle or blood where she was last seen alive and her stepfather had an iron-clad alibi once the police got around to investigating things a little more thoroughly. And, of course, even after two decades there has been no sign of her body.'

Kellie was still frowning. 'So after all these years Ruth doesn't really know if her daughter is alive or dead?' she asked.

'No, but, as I said, she lives in hope.'

'But that's awful!' she said. 'At least when my mum died we had a few months' warning. I miss her terribly but at least I know where she is. I was there when she took her last breath and I was there when the coffin was lowered in the ground.'

Matt felt his gut clench but fought against it. 'What did your mother die of?' he asked.

'Pancreatic cancer,' she said. 'She became jaundiced over-night and started vomiting and within three days we had the diagnosis.'

'How long did she have?'

'Five months,' she said. 'I took time off from my surgical term to nurse her. She died in my arms…'

Matt felt a lump the size of a boulder lodge in his throat. 'At least you were there,' he said, his tone sounding rough around the edges. 'Spouses and relatives don't always get there in time.'

'Yes…' she said, looking down at her hands. 'At least I was there…'

Silence followed for several minutes.

'So where did you go on the weekend?' Kellie asked.

Matt's hands tightened fractionally on the steering-wheel. 'I went to visit some…' He paused briefly over the word. 'Friends in Brisbane. It was their daughter's thirtieth birthday.'

'It was my birthday a week ago,' Kellie said. 'I'm twenty-nine—the big one is next year. I'm kind of dreading it, to tell you the truth. My family wants me to have a big party but I'm not sure I want to go to all that fuss.' She swung her gaze his way again. 'So was your friend's daughter's party a big celebration?'

His eyes were trained on the road ahead but Kellie noticed he was gripping the steering-wheel as if it was a lifeline. 'No,' he said. 'It was very small.'

Another silence ticked away.

'How old are your brothers?' Matt broke it by asking.

'Alistair and Josh are twins,' she said. 'They're four years younger than me at twenty-five. Sebastian, but we always call him Seb, is twenty-three, Nick's twenty and Cain is nineteen.'

'Do they all still live at home?'

'Yes and no,' she said. 'They're a bit like homing pigeons—or maybe more like locusts—swooping in, eating all the food and then moving on again.'

Matt noticed her fond smile and marvelled at the difference between his life and hers. He had grown up as an only child to parents who had eventually divorced when he'd been seven. He had never quite forgiven his mother for leaving his father with a small child to rear. And his father had never quite forgiven him for being a small, dependent, somewhat insecure and shy boy, which had made things even more difficult and strained between them. He couldn't remember the last time he had spoken to either of his parents. They hadn't even met Madeleine.

'What about you?' Kellie asked. 'Do you have brothers or sisters?'

'No.'

'Are both your parents still alive?'

'Yes.'

'Do you ever answer a question with more than one word?' she asked.

The distance between his brows decreased. 'When I think it's appropriate,' he said.

'You're not the easiest person to talk to,' she said. 'I'm used to living in a household of six men where I have to shout to get a word in edgeways, unless they're in one of their non-communicative moods. Talking to you is like getting blood out of a stone.'

Matt felt his shoulders tensing. 'I'm not a chit-chat person. If you don't like it, tough. Find someone else's ear to chew off.'

She sent him a reproachful look. 'The least you could do is make some sort of an effort to make me feel at home here. This is a big thing for me. I'm the one who's put myself out to come here to fill a vacancy, a vacancy, I might add, that isn't generally easy to fill. Outback postings are notoriously diffi-cult to attract doctors to, especially given the timeframe of this one. You should be grateful I've put my hand up so willingly. Not many people would.'

'I am very grateful, Dr Thorne, but I had absolutely nothing to do with your appointment and I have some serious doubts about your suitability.'

'*What?*' she said, with an affronted glare. 'Who are you to decide whether I'm suitable or not?'

'I think you've been sent here for the wrong reasons,' he said.

Kellie frowned at him. 'The wrong reasons? What on earth do you mean? I'm a GP with all the right qualifications and I've worked in a busy practice in Newcastle for four years.'

He was still looking at the road ahead but she noticed his knuckles were now almost white where he was gripping the steering-wheel. 'This is a rough-and-tough area,' he said. 'You're probably used to the sort of facilities that are just not available out here. Sometimes we lose patients not because of their injuries or illnesses but because we can't get them to help in time. We do what we can with what we've got, but it can do in even the most level-headed person at times.'

Kellie totally understood where he was coming from. She had met plenty of paramedics and trauma surgeons during her various terms to know that working at the coal face of tragedy was no picnic. But she had toughened up over the years of her training and with the help of her friends and family had come to a point in her life where she felt compelled to do her bit in spite of the sleepless nights that resulted. She had wanted to be a doctor all her life. She loved taking care of people and what better way to do that than out in the bush where patients were not just patients but friends as well?

'Contrary to what you think, I believe I'll manage just fine,' she said. 'But if you think it's so rough and tough out here, why have you stayed here so long?'

'I would hardly describe six years as a long time,' he said, without glancing her way.

'Are you planning to stay here indefinitely?' she asked.

'It depends.'

'On what?'

He threw her an irritated look. 'Has anyone ever told you you ask too many questions?'

Kellie bristled with anger. 'Well, *sor-ry* for trying to be friendly. Sheesh! You take the quiet, silent type to a whole new level.'

He let out a sigh and sent her a quick, unreadable glance. 'Look, it's been a long, tiring weekend. All I can think about right now is getting home and going to bed.'

'Do you live alone?' she asked.

His eyes flickered upwards, his hands still tight on the steering-wheel. 'Yes.'

Kellie looked out at the dusty, arid landscape; even the red river gums lining the road looked gnarled with thirst. 'I guess this isn't such a great place to meet potential partners,' she mused. Swivelling her head to look at him again, she added, 'I read this article in a women's magazine about men in the bush and how hard it is for them to find a wife. It's not like in the city where there are clubs and pubs and gyms and so on. Out here it's just miles and miles of bush between neighbours and towns.'

'I'm not interested in finding a wife,' he said with an implacable edge to his tone.

'It seems a pretty bleak existence,' she remarked as the tiny township came into view. 'Don't you want more for your life?'

His dark blue eyes collided with hers. 'If you don't like it here, there's another plane out at five p.m. on Saturday.'

She sent him a determined look. 'I am here for six months, Dr McNaught, so you'd better get used to it. I'm not a quitter and even though you are the most unfriendly colleague I've ever met, I'm not going to be run out of town just because you have a chip on your shoulder about women.'

His brows snapped together irritably. 'I do not have a chip on my shoulder about women.'

Kellie tossed her head and looked out at the small strip of shops that lined both sides of the impossibly wide street. It was certainly nothing like she was used to, even though Newcastle was nowhere near the size of Sydney or Melbourne, or even for that matter Brisbane.

Culwulla Creek had little more than a general store, which was now closed, a small hardware centre, a hamburger café, a service station, a tiny school and a rundown-looking pub that was currently booming with business.

'The clinic is just over there in that small cottage,' Matt said, pointing to the left-hand side of the road just before the pub. 'I'll get Trish to show you around in the next day or so once you've settled in at the Montgomerys' house.'

As they drove past the pub, people were spilling out on the street, stubbies of beer in hand, squinting against the late afternoon sunlight.

'G'day, Dr McNaught,' one man wearing an acubra hat and a cast on his right arm called out. 'How was your weekend in the big smoke?'

'Shut up, Bluey,' another man said, elbowing his mate in the ribs.

Matt slowed the car down and leaned forward slightly to look past Kellie in the passenger seat. 'It was fine. How's your arm?'

The man with the hat lifted his can of beer with his other arm and grinned. 'I can still hold my beer so I must be all right.'

Kellie witnessed the first genuine smile crack Matt's face and her heart did a funny little jerk behind her chest wall. His dark blue eyes crinkled up at the corners, his lean jaw relaxed and his usually furrowed brow smoothed out, making his already attractive features heart-stoppingly gorgeous.

'Take it easy, Bluey,' he said, still smiling. 'It was a bad break and you'll need the full six weeks to rest it.'

'I'm resting it,' Bluey assured him, and peered through the passenger window. 'So who's the little lady?'

'This is Dr Thorne,' Matt said, his smile instantly disappearing. 'She's the new locum.'

Kellie lifted her hand in a fingertip wave. 'Hi, there.'

Bluey's light blue eyes twinkled. 'G'day, Dr Thorne. How about joining us for a drink to get to know the locals?'

'I have to get her settled into Tim and Claire's house,' Matt said before Kellie could respond. 'She has a lot of baggage.'

Kellie glowered at him before turning back to smile at Bluey. 'I would love to join you all,' she said. 'What time does the pub close?'

Bluey grinned from ear to ear. 'We'll keep it open just for you, Dr Thorne.'

Matt drove on past the tiny church and cemetery before turning right into a pepper corn-tree-lined street. 'Tim and Claire's house is the cream one,' he said. 'The car will be in the garage.'

Kellie looked at the cottage with interest and trepidation.

It was a three-bedroom weatherboard with a corrugated-tin roof, a large rainwater tank on one side and a shady verandah wrapped around the outside of the house. There was no garden to speak of, but not for want of trying, she observed as she noted the spindly skeletons of what looked to be some yellowed sweet peas clinging listlessly to the mid-height picket fence. There were several pots on the verandah that had suffered much the same fate, and the patchy and parched lawn looked as if it could do with a long soak and a decent trim. There were other similar cottages further along the street, although both of the houses either side of the Montgomerys' appeared to be vacant.

Fixing an I-can-get-through-this-for-six-months expression on her face, Kellie rummaged for the keys she had been sent in the post as Matt began to unload the luggage. She walked up to the front door and searched through the array of keys to find the right one, but with little success. She was down to the last three when she felt Matt come up behind her.

'Here,' he said. 'Let me.'

Kellie felt the brush of his arm against her waist as he took the keys and her heart did another little uncoordinated skip in her chest. She watched as his long, tanned fingers selected the right key and inserted it into the lock, turning it effortlessly before pushing the door open for her.

'You go in and have a look around while I bring in your bags,' he said as he opened the meter box near the door and turned a switch. 'The hot water will take a couple of hours to heat but everything else should be OK. There's an air-conditioning control panel in the lounge, which serves the main living area of the house.'

Kellie looked guiltily towards his car where her bags were

lined up behind the open hatchback. 'I don't expect you to be my slave,' she said. 'I can carry my own bags inside.'

'Then you must be a whole lot stronger than you look because I nearly bulged a disc loading them in there in the first place.'

She put her hands on her hips as if she was admonishing one of her younger brothers. 'I *am* here for half a year, you know,' she said. 'I need lots of stuff, especially out here.'

'I hate to be the one to tell you this but the sort of stuff you need to survive out here can't be packed into four hot pink suitcases, Dr Thorne,' Matt said, stepping back down off the verandah to his car.

'What *is* it with you?' she asked, following him to his car in quick angry strides. 'You seem determined to turn me off this appointment before I've even started.'

Matt carried two of her cases to the verandah as she yapped at his heels like a small terrier. She was exactly what this town didn't need, he thought. No, strike that—she was exactly what *he* didn't need right now. He wasn't ready. He wondered if he ever would be ready and yet…

'Give me that bag,' she demanded. *'Now.'*

Matt mentally rolled his eyes. She looked so fierce standing there with her hands on her slim-as-a-boy's hips, her toffee-brown eyes flashing. For a tiny moment she reminded him of…

He gave himself a hard mental slap and handed her one of the bags. 'I'll bring in the rest,' he said. 'And watch out for snakes as you go in.'

She stopped in mid-stride, her hand falling away from the handle of her bag. 'Snakes?' she asked. 'You mean…' She visibly gulped. 'Inside?'

CHAPTER FOUR

'SNAKES are attracted to water,' he said as he picked up another one of her bags. 'This has been one of the longest droughts in history. They can slink in under doors in search of a dripping tap. One of the locals had one come in under the door a few blocks from here. They lost their Jack Russell terrier as a result. I just thought I'd warn you. It's better to be safe than sorry.'

Kellie eyed the open front door with wide, uncertain eyes. Snakes were fine in their place, which for her had up until this point been behind a thick sheet of glass at a zoological park. She had never met one in the wild, and had certainly never envisaged meeting one in her living space. She was OK with rats and mice; she was even fine with spiders—but *snakes*?

She suppressed a little shudder and straightened her shoulders as she faced him coming up the verandah steps with a bag in each hand. 'I suppose the next thing you'll be telling me is the house is haunted.'

Something shifted at the back of his eyes. 'No, it's not haunted,' he said, and moved past her to take the bags he was carrying to one of the bedrooms off the passage.

Kellie followed him gingerly down the hallway, her eyes darting sideways for any sign of a black or brown coil lying in wait to strike, but to her immense relief nothing seemed to be amiss. It looked and felt like any other house that had been unoccupied for a while—the air a little hot and stale and the blinds down over the windows, which added to the general sense of abandonment.

The sudden wave of homesickness that assailed her was almost overwhelming. A house was meant to be a home but it couldn't be that without people in it and she—for the next few months—was going to be the only person inside this house.

It was a daunting thought, Kellie realised as she wandered into the kitchen. The layout was modern but very basic, as if Tim and Claire Montgomery had not wanted to waste money on top-notch appliances and joinery.

The rest of the house was similar, tasteful but modestly decorated, the furniture a little dated though comfortable-looking.

Matt came back in with the last of her bags and put them in the largest of the three bedrooms before he came back out to the sitting room where she was trying to undo one of the two windows. 'What's the problem?' he asked.

'I want to air the house but I think this window is stuck,' she said giving it another rattle.

'Here, let me have a go.'

Kellie stepped back as he worked on the latch and pushed the window upwards with his shoulder, the timber frame creaking in protest.

'It needs to be shaved back a bit,' he said, inspecting the inner section of the window. 'I'll send someone around to fix it for you.'

'Thanks, I'd appreciate it.'

He reached into his back pocket and took out his wallet. Flipping it open, he pulled out a business card and handed it to her. 'Here are my home and mobile and the clinic numbers.'

Kellie caught a brief glimpse of a photograph of a young woman just before he closed his wallet. 'Who is that?' she asked.

His expression closed down and his tone was guarded and clipped as he responded, 'Who is who?'

'The woman in your wallet,' she said.

His brows moved together in a frown. 'Do you make it a habit of prying into people's wallets?' he asked.

'I wasn't prying,' she protested. 'You had it open so I looked.'

'Would you like to count how much money I have in there while you're at it, Dr Thorne?' he asked with a sardonic curl of his lip.

Kellie glared up at him. 'If that is your girlfriend in your wallet then I don't know what on earth she sees in you,' she said. 'You're the most obnoxiously unfriendly man I've ever met and let me tell you I've met plenty. I just didn't realise I had to travel quite this far to meet yet another one.'

Blue eyes battled with brown in a crackling-with-tension silence that seemed to go on indefinitely.

Kellie was determined not to look away first. She was used to the stare-downs of her brothers but something about Matthew McNaught's midnight-blue gaze as it wrestled with hers caught her off guard. She found herself blushing and averted her head in case he saw it. 'Thank you for the lift and bringing in my bags,' she said in a curt tone. 'No doubt I'll see you at the clinic some time.'

'Yes, I expect you will.' His tone was equally brusque.

Kellie listened as his footsteps echoed down the hall. She heard the screen door squeak open and close and then the creak of the weathered timber of the verandah as he stepped on it before going down the three steps leading to the pathway to the gate. She heard his car start then the grab of the wheels on the gravel as he backed out of the driveway and the growl of the diesel engine as he drove back the way they had come, turning right, away from town at the corner.

And then all Kellie could hear was the sound of her own breathing. It seemed faster than normal and her heart felt like it was skipping every now and again just to keep up.

She turned from the window and looked at the space where moments before Matt had been standing, frowning at her, those incredibly blue eyes searing and yet shadowed at the same time…

A sudden knock on the front door made her nearly jump out of her skin but when she heard Ruth Williams's friendly voice calling out, her panic quickly subsided. 'Dr Thorne? I managed to get some milk and bread for you. I rang Cheryl Yates who runs the general store and she made up a survival pack for you. You can pay her later.'

Kellie pushed open the screen door. 'That was very thoughtful of you both.'

'Not at all,' Ruth said, handing over the basket of groceries.

'Please come in,' Kellie said. 'I'm still finding my way around but I can rustle us up a cup of tea if you'd like one.'

'I would love one,' Ruth said, puffing slightly. 'I think Cheryl's even put some of those fancy teabags in here somewhere and some chocolate biscuits. You'd better put them in the fridge, though, as this heat would melt stone.'

'Yes, it is rather hot, isn't it?' Kellie answered as she led the way to the kitchen. 'But I'm sure I'll get used to it in a day or two.'

'You know when you first stepped off the plane with Dr McNaught I thought I was seeing a ghost,' Ruth said as she started to help unpack the groceries.

Kellie turned and looked at her. 'A ghost?'

Ruth's smile had a hint of sadness about it. 'Yes. Although

your hair is a different colour, you reminded me a bit of Madeleine,' she said, 'Dr McNaught's fiancée.'

Kellie felt her eyes widen in surprise. No wonder he'd said he wasn't looking for a wife, although she couldn't imagine who would be brave enough to take him on. 'Dr McNaught is engaged?' she asked.

'Was engaged,' Ruth corrected. 'She was killed in an accident two days before their wedding.'

'Oh, dear…' Kellie said, a wave of sympathy washing over her, followed by a rising tide of insight into why Matt was so standoffish and formal. She mentally cringed at his dislike of her prying into the photograph in his wallet.

'He doesn't talk about it much, of course,' Ruth went on. 'But that's the male way, isn't it?'

Kellie nibbled at her lip. 'Yes…yes, it certainly is…'

Ruth handed her a carton of milk. 'It was her birthday on Saturday,' she said. 'That's why he went to Brisbane—to visit her parents.'

'That was nice of him,' Kellie offered, still feeling utterly wretched about her rapid judgement of him.

Ruth gave her another sad smile. 'Yes, he does it every year.'

Kellie put the milk in the fridge and filled the kettle before she sat down opposite the older lady. 'Dr McNaught told me about your daughter,' she said. 'It must be very hard for you…you know, not knowing where Tegan is or what happened to her.'

Ruth let out a little sigh. 'It is hard,' she said. 'The hardest thing after all this time is that no one is actively searching for her any more. I feel that I'll go to my grave without knowing what happened to her.'

'The police keep most missing-person files open, though, don't they?' Kellie said. 'I've seen a few news stories about old cases that have been solved, using DNA to match perpetrators to crimes.'

'That's true,' Ruth said, 'but out here there isn't the manpower to do any more than maintain law and order. Doctors aren't the only people who resist remote country appointments— police are pretty thin on the ground out here, too.'

Kellie met the older woman's brown eyes. 'You don't believe she's dead, do you?' she asked.

Ruth held her gaze for several moments. 'No,' she said. 'I feel it in here.' She placed a hand over her heart. 'She's out there somewhere, I just know it.'

Kellie felt deeply for the poor woman. She had a pretty clear idea of the process of denial—she had witnessed it in her father for the last six years. He still acted as if her mother was going to walk in the door. He even occasionally spoke of her in the present tense, which made the job of getting on with his life so much harder for him and his family, not to mention Aunty Kate.

'Well, I must let you settle in,' Ruth said a few minutes later after they had finished the tea. 'It's an isolated place out here—but it's not an unfriendly one.'

'I'm very glad to hear that,' Kellie said with genuine feeling. 'This is a leap into the unknown for me. I'm right out of my comfort zone but I need the challenge right now.'

'Well, it will certainly be challenging, it always is when the unexpected happens in places as far out as this,' Ruth said as she gathered up her bag. 'But Matthew McNaught is a very capable doctor. He's experienced and caring. I am sure you'll enjoy working with him, especially once you get to know him. This last weekend was a tough one for him. It'll take him a few days to get back to normal.'

'I think we'll get along just fine,' she said to the older

woman with a smile. 'In any case, I've got a week up my sleeve to get a feel for the place. I kind of figured it would be wise not to rush headlong into a close community like this.'

'You might not have any choice, my dear,' Ruth said with a sombre look. 'Things can happen out here in a blink of an eye.'

Soon after Ruth left Kellie decided to walk the short distance to the pub. She had always enjoyed male company and while the pub looked nothing like the family-friendly bistros she was used to, she didn't see any harm in getting to know some of the locals in a relaxed and casual atmosphere.

She was barely in the door before Bluey, the man with the broken arm, came ambling over. 'What would you like to drink, Doc?'

Kellie smiled so as not to offend him. 'It's fine, really. I'll get my own.'

'Nah,' he drawled as he winked at his two mates. 'It's been a long time since I bought a pretty lady a drink. Don't spoil it for me. What'll you have?'

Kellie agreed to have a lemonade, lime and bitters and sat at the table with Bluey and his cronies, who turned out to be two other farmers looking as though they had spent many a long day in the sun.

'So what brings a nice girl like you out to a place like this?' Jeff, the oldest of the three, asked.

'I saw Tim Montgomery's advertisement in the *Australian Medical Journal* and thought it would be a great chance to do my bit for the bush,' she answered. 'A house, a car and a job all rolled into one sounded too good to miss.'

'It sounds too good to be true, right, Jeff?' Bluey said with a gap-toothed grin.

Kellie wasn't sure what he meant and didn't have time to

ask as just then she heard a commotion from behind the counter of the pub.

'Quick, call the doctor!' a female voice shrieked. 'I think I've cut off my finger!'

Kellie leapt to her feet and approached the bar. 'Can I help?' she asked. 'I'm a doctor.'

The face of Bruce, the barman, was ashen as the woman was clutching a blood-soaked teatowel to her right hand. 'It looks pretty bad,' he said. 'Perhaps I'd better call Matt McNaught.'

Kellie stood her ground. 'By the time Dr McNaught gets here I could at least stem the bleeding and assess the damage.'

'Good point, but I'll give him a call in any case. He'll know what to do, you being new in town and all,' Bruce said, and lifted a section of the bar to allow her access to where the woman was sitting visibly shaking as she cradled her hand against her chest.

Kellie introduced herself to the woman, Julie Smithton, who told her she had been using a sharp knife to cut up some lemons when the knife had slipped and cut through the top of her finger.

'Let me have a look at the damage,' Kellie said, gently taking the woman's hand in hers. She carefully unpeeled the teatowel to find a deep laceration across the palmar surface, indicating there was a possibility the flexor tendon could be severed.

'Have I cut it off?' Julie asked in a thread-like voice.

Kellie smiled reassuringly. 'No, Julie, you haven't. The finger's completely intact. But it looks like you might have damaged a tendon. Do you think you can try and bend your finger, like this?' She demonstrated the action of moving her index finger up and down in a wave-like action.

Julie gingerly lifted her hand but even though she was clearly trying to move her finger there was no flexion response. 'I can't do it,' she cried.

'It's all right,' Kellie said gently. 'It's something that can be easily fixed with a bit of microsurgery. You'll be back to normal in no time.'

Julie's eyes flared in fear. 'Microsurgery?'

'Yes,' Kellie said. 'It's done by a plastic surgeon, but it will soon be—'

'But can't Dr McNaught do it?' Julie asked. 'I don't want to travel all the way to Brisbane. I've got three kids.'

'Who's looking after them now?' Kellie asked.

Julie lowered her eyes. 'They're on their own at the house,' she mumbled. 'They're not little kids any more. I guess they might be all right for a day or so.'

'What about their father?' Kellie asked. 'Couldn't he look after them?'

A dark, embittered look came into the young woman's eyes. 'He left us close to three years ago. Got himself a new family now in Charleville, last I heard.'

Kellie looked at the woman's prematurely lined and weather-beaten face and wondered how old she was. She wasn't sure but she didn't think she was that old, but clearly the strain of bringing up three children on her own had taken its toll, not to mention the unforgiving outback climate.

'You'll only be in hospital a few days, five at the most,' Kellie said. Turning to the hovering Bruce, she asked, 'Do you have a first-aid kit here, Bruce? My doctor's bag is back at the cottage. And I'll need the number of the flying doctor service. I left the card Dr McNaught gave me with all the contact numbers on it back at the cottage.'

Once the call had been made Julie asked to be taken to her

house to see her kids and organise things before the flying doctor arrived.

'I'll take you,' Bluey offered as he came to where they were gathered.

'Yeah, right,' Julie said with a look of disdain. 'You're exactly what I need right now, a broken-armed drunk to come to my rescue in a beat-up hulk of a car.'

Bluey looked affronted. 'I'm no drunk, Jules. I've only had two light stubbies. Sure, there's a spot of rust or two in the old Holden, but I can drive it with one arm tied behind my back...' he grinned and added, 'or my front.'

'What's going on?' Matt's voice sounded deep and controlled as he came in, carrying a doctor's bag in one hand.

'Julie has a lacerated flexor tendon and I've organised transport to Brisbane with the flying doctor service,' Kellie informed him. 'I called them and they're only half an hour away on another trip from the station out at Gunnawanda Gully.'

Matt took Kellie aside and, looking down at her seriously asked, 'I notice you have blood on your hands,' he said. 'Do you realise you should be wearing gloves? You could put yourself at risk of infection.'

Kellie felt a little tremor of unease pass through her. 'I didn't have my doctor's bag with me,' she said. 'I simply responded to a call for help and acted accordingly.'

'There's no point putting yourself at risk,' he admonished her. 'Once you had established it wasn't a life-threatening injury you should have taken universal precautions. You should have called me and met me at the clinic where we could have explored the wound, gloved up at the very least.'

'I realise that but—'

'Furthermore, if it turns out Mrs Smithton doesn't have a tendon injury, you would have wasted thousands of dollars of community money, getting an air ambulance out here for nothing.'

Kellie was incensed. She knew a tendon injury when she saw one—her brother Seb had severed his during an ice-hockey match when he'd been sixteen—so she considered herself somewhat of an expert on that particular injury.

'Not only that…' Matt was still dressing her down like a junior colleague. 'You are not officially on duty until next week.'

'I don't see why that should make any—'

Matt ignored her to turn back to the group surrounding Julie. He opened his bag and, putting on some surgical gloves, gently inspected the wound. 'What about if I call Ruth Williams?' he asked Julie. 'She'll be happy to help you out with the boys.'

'I called her a few minutes ago,' Bruce piped up. 'She's gone to the house to get some things together for Julie for the hospital. She said she'll meet you at the airstrip.'

'Good,' Matt said, and stripped off his gloves. 'You'll be OK, Julie. It's a bit of bad luck but it could have been a lot worse.'

'I don't see how,' Julie said with a despondent set to her features. 'I won't be able to work for a couple of weeks and I need the money right now.'

Matt put his hand on her shoulder and gently squeezed. 'The boys will be fine, Julie. Ruth will love being with them, don't worry. I'll keep my eye on things as well, OK?'

Julie gave him a grateful look. 'The new doctor's nice, isn't she?' she said. 'Very pretty too, don't you think?'

Matt concentrated on zipping up his doctor's bag. 'I hadn't really noticed.'

Kellie felt that all too familiar ache of inadequacy as she overheard the exchange. Maybe she should do something about her hair, she thought, tucking a wayward strand behind one ear. A few highlights, maybe even a trim, or even a new style would give her ego a much-needed boost. Not that she'd noticed a hairdresser's anywhere in town. Culwulla Creek was hardly the place to prepare for a Miss Universe line-up, Kellie realised, but a girl—even a girl living in the dry dusty outback—needed a lift now and again, didn't she?

'I think she's just what this town needs,' Julie said. 'Tim and Claire will be delighted to know they chose exactly the right person to fill the position.'

'The flying doctor's just landed,' Bluey announced as he popped his head around the door. 'Do you want me to come with you and hold your hand, Jules?' he asked. 'I've got nothing planned for the next few days.'

Julie gave him another scornful look. 'That'd be the blind leading the blind, wouldn't it?'

Bluey grinned boyishly. 'You break me up, Jules.'

Kellie looked at Matt, who was smiling at the exchange. It wasn't a broad smile by any stretch of the imagination but it was enough to make his dark blue eyes crinkle up at the corners and his normally rigid mouth relax. Kellie couldn't help thinking how sensual it looked without its tightened contours.

He turned and caught her staring at him and his smile instantly faded. 'Is there something wrong, Dr Thorne?' he asked.

Kellie met his gaze. 'No,' she said, suddenly feeling a little embarrassed under his frowning scrutiny.

He held her look for a tense moment. 'Excuse me,' he said. 'I have a patient to see to. I'll let you get back to your socialising.'

Kellie couldn't help thinking there was a hint of criticism in his tone. He made it sound as if she had nothing better to do than sit around and drink cocktails with the locals while he got on with the job of being the only reliable, hard-working doctor in town. 'I'd like to come with you to the airstrip,' she said with a little jut of her chin. 'I need to learn the ropes and now is as good a time as any.'

He looked as if he was about to disagree, but perhaps because of the assembled group nearby he appeared to change his mind. 'All right,' he said, letting out a sigh that sounded like something between irritation and resignation. 'Follow me.'

CHAPTER FIVE

KELLIE thought the airstrip looked even smaller than when she had arrived there only hours earlier. The arrivals building was no bigger than a suburban garden shed, and the red gravel runway looked too small for a car to brake suddenly, let alone an aircraft.

Before the plane had landed a team of locals had performed the mandatory 'roo shoo' which involved a couple of cars driving up and down the strip to clear away any wildlife such as kangaroos, emus or possums. Kellie could see one or two of the drivers standing chatting to the pilot as she and Matt approached.

Once Julie was settled on board, Brian King, the pilot, Nathan Curtis, the doctor, and Fran Bradley, the nurse, quickly introduced themselves.

'It's great to meet you,' Fran said with a friendly smile. 'I know of a few women out on the land who'll be glad to know you've joined the outback clinic team.'

Kellie swallowed as she looked at the aircraft. 'Er…yes, I'm sure it will be heaps of fun…'

'Dr Thorne isn't too keen on flying,' Matt said with an unreadable expression.

Kellie glowered at him. 'I'm sure I'll get used to it if it's not too rough.' She turned back to the nurse. 'I had a scary trip back from a rotation I did in Tamworth a few years ago. We had to make an emergency landing when one of the engines failed. A few of the passengers were seriously injured. I'm afraid I've been a bit of a coward ever since.'

Brian smiled reassuringly. 'We'll do our best to keep you safe out here,' he said. 'We don't take unnecessary risks. I've only had to make one emergency landing in twenty years of flying in the outback.'

'That's very good to know,' Kellie said, with another nervous glance towards the plane which, in her opinion, looked like it wouldn't look out of place in a child's toybox.

Julie was soon loaded on board and everyone stood back as the engine turned over in preparation for take-off. On the way back to his car Matt stopped to chat to Ruth. 'Are you sure you'll be able to manage Julie's boys?' he asked with a concerned pleat of his brow.

'I'll be fine,' Ruth assured him. 'They'll keep me on my toes, no doubt, but it will be good for me. Take my mind off things.'

'Can I help in any way?' Kellie asked. 'It's not as if I'm not used to handling boys and I don't start at the clinic until next week.'

'If you'd like to, that would be lovely,' Ruth said. 'Julie's house is on Commercial Road, number fifteen, I think it is from memory—no one really bothers with numbers out here. Anyway, it's the house next door to the old community centre.'

'I'll find it,' Kellie said with a confident smile.

Matt opened the car door for Kellie once Ruth had driven off. 'You may have had plenty of experience handling your brothers but I can assure you Julie's boys are something else. They've been running wild for years. I've had each of them for patients with every injury imaginable. How one of them hasn't been killed before now is little short of a miracle.'

Kellie waited until he was behind the wheel before asking, 'How old are they?'

He frowned as if searching his memory. 'Ty is fifteen, Rowan fourteen and Cade is twelve.'

'And how old is Julie?'

'She's not long turned thirty-one, I think.'

Kellie lifted her brows. 'Gosh, she did start young. She was, what, just sixteen when she had the oldest boy.'

'Yes, but out here that's not unusual,' he said. 'I have several patients who are teenage mothers. It's tough on them as they can't really get out of the cycle of poverty without an education to fall back on. They end up having a couple more kids and living on welfare for years on end.'

Kellie couldn't help thinking of how different her life had been in spite of her mother's untimely death. She at least had been able to complete her training even while juggling her father's and brothers' needs. She hadn't really realised until now how lucky she was to have done so. She could so easily have chosen another path, like so many others did in times of grief and trauma.

'Ruth told me about your fiancée,' she said after a lengthy silence. 'I'm sorry...I didn't realise how tough this weekend must have been for you.'

All the air inside the car seemed to be sucked out on the harshly indrawn breath he took. 'It's fine,' he said. 'I'm over it. Life moves on. It has to.'

Kellie glanced at his white-knuckled grip on the steering-wheel and wondered if that was entirely true. He reminded her of her father, stoic and grittily determined to ignore how much life had changed, pretending he was coping when each day another part of him seemed to shrivel up and die.

'What did she do?' she asked, after she'd let another little silence pass. 'Was she a doctor, like you?'

'No,' he said, staring at the road ahead. 'She was a teacher.'

'What grade?'

'First grade.'

'How did you meet?'

He glanced at her as if he found her questions both annoying and intrusive. 'We went to school together.' He looked forward again and paused for a second or two before adding, 'We dated since senior high school.'

Oh, boy, Kellie thought. Losing a childhood sweetheart was a tough call. So many memories were intertwined. It was almost impossible to move forward without some sort of survival guilt. Her father was living proof of it. He and her mother had met on the first day of high school and had never had eyes for anyone else but each other.

Kellie, on the other hand, had had plenty of casual male relationships during her adolescence but after her mother had died her only serious relationship had been with Harley Edwards. It worried her that with just under a year until she turned thirty she was way behind her peers in terms of experience. But with the responsibilities of juggling both her studies and her needy family she hadn't had time to socialise in the same way her peers had done.

When Harley had come along, with his easygoing charm, she hadn't given the relationship enough thought before she had committed herself to being his lover. She had known enough about her body and its responses to know she had often been a little short-changed when it had come to their very occasional intimate moments. She had always put it down to overwork and tiredness on her part, but after feeling the fine sandpaper-like touch of Matt McNaught's hands earlier, she wondered if had more to do with not meeting the right person.

She glanced at Matt's hands again and suppressed a tiny shiver. They looked like the sort of hands that would know their way around a woman's body. Long fingered and strong, capable and yet gentle when he needed to be. She had seen that when he had examined Julie's wound earlier.

'Look, if you're really not keen about flying out here, I'm quite happy to do the remote clinics while you hold the fort in town,' Matt said into the silence. 'I hadn't realised you'd had such a frightening experience. An emergency landing would be enough to shake anyone's confidence.'

Kellie felt her heart swell at his gesture of consideration for her feelings. 'Thank you, but I really think I need to conquer my demons,' she said. 'That's part of the reason I came out here. I hate being beaten by something. I knew it would be tough and that there would be flying involved, but patients have to take priority over personal feelings, right?'

He met her gaze briefly. 'Out here patients always take priority,' he said. 'Our feelings don't come into it at all.'

'I guess they don't if you've got them locked away so tightly no one can even get close,' she commented wryly.

His mouth tightened into a flat white line. 'If I choose not to wear my heart on my sleeve, that's surely my business and no one else's,' he said in a curt tone. 'Ruth had no right to tell you all the details of my private life. She was way out of line.'

'She cares for you,' Kellie countered. 'In fact, I think she understands more than most what you're going through.'

He was still looking straight ahead. 'I suppose you mean because we've both lost someone we loved.'

'Yes. She's a mother who has lost her daughter,' she said. 'You're a man who has lost his fiancée. You have a lot of common ground. Grief is a great leveller—sure, we experience it in different ways but it's still grief. Take Julie, for instance. She's lost the father of her children, not from death but because her husband decided he wanted something other than what she could offer. She's left to bring up three boys on her own. In some ways she might have coped better if her husband had died rather than being left to live with the stigma of being rejected for another woman.'

Matt frowned as he thought about what Kellie had said. He had tried over the years to move on from his grief and each year he felt as if he had taken a few more important steps away from it. But then as Madeleine's birthday crept up on him each October he felt the guilt start to gnaw at him, like a tiny pebble inside one of his shoes. It didn't help that Madeleine's parents expected him to be the same broken man he had been six years ago.

For the first time since he had been travelling to Brisbane each year, Matt had felt like a fraud. He had felt almost sickened this time by the way John and Mary Donaldson persisted in maintaining their daughter's bedroom like a shrine to her memory. It was as if Madeleine's parents had never quite accepted their daughter was finally gone. Madeleine's clothes were still hanging in the wardrobe, even her wedding dress and veil this time had reminded Matt of that scene out of Charles Dickens' *Great Expectations* where the jilted Miss Haversham lived in a constant state of wearing her wedding finery, even as it creased and rotted around her aging form.

Madeleine's bed was still made up as if she was coming home to slip in between the neatly pressed sheets, her school trophies and certificates and university degree were on the wall, and her bedside clock was plugged in as if her slim hand would reach out and switch off the alarm the next morning…

Matt gripped the steering-wheel even tighter, fighting against the groundswell of feeling rising inside him. He realised it wasn't grief but frustration that Madeleine's parents were not just holding onto their daughter, but to him as well. 'I'm dealing with it in my own way and in my own time,' he said. 'I don't like talking about it—it brings it all back.'

'I felt the same about my mother's death for ages,' Kellie said. 'I could barely mention her name. But I've come to realise it's much healthier to deal with what you're feeling at the time rather than push it aside. It festers under the surface otherwise, and you can't move on with your life.'

'As a child, no matter what age you are, you more or less expect to outlive your parents,' he said tightly. 'It's not the same thing at all, losing the person you were expecting to marry a couple of days later. There are issues that crop up from time to time, reminders, that sort of thing. It never seems to go away.'

Kellie took a moment to absorb what he'd said to consider if she agreed with it or not. Losing her mother had been devastating. It had been devastating for her father and brothers as well as it had come right out of the blue. One moment their forty-seven-year-old active and energetic mother had been happy and healthy, doing all the things loving mothers did, and the next she had been diagnosed with a terminal illness.

It had felt at the time like the family had suddenly slammed head first into a brick wall. Life was never going to be the same again and each of them had known it. Yes, they'd had a few months to say what had needed to be said so their mother could die in peace, but it hadn't really lessened the grief. If anything, it had prolonged it, as they had watched her waste away before their eyes, each of them watching helplessly until she'd taken her final breath and slipped away.

'I'm not sure I totally agree with you,' she said. 'I miss my mother terribly. There are still days when I reach for my phone to call or text her about something and then I realise she's not here any more. I know for a fact it will get worse if or when I become a mother myself. I have my father, of course, who is absolutely wonderful but no one can ever replace your mother.'

'Yes, well, I've managed without one for the last twenty-six years so I'm not sure I totally agree with you,' he returned.

Kellie looked at the embittered set of what she could see of his features as he continued to focus fixedly on the road ahead. 'You lost your mother when you were a kid?' she asked, frowning.

'She left when I was seven,' he said taking the turn into the street where the Montgomerys' cottage was situated. 'Apart from the occasional birthday card and cheap Christmas present up until I was about ten, I haven't seen or heard from her since.'

'I'm sorry to hear that,' she said, biting her lip as she thought of how hurt he must have felt at such a young age. Her experience with her younger brothers made her very much aware of how incredibly sensitive young boys were. They hid it to protect themselves but it didn't mean they were incapable of deep feelings.

'What about your father?' she asked.

'My father?' His mouth twisted cynically. 'My father still likes to think if it hadn't been for me my mother wouldn't have run off with another man. The burden of looking after a small child, or so he thinks, was the reason she took off for greener pastures. I see him when duty calls, which basically means when he runs short of money, but other than that I keep my distance.'

'That's so sad,' she said with deep sincerity. 'Do you have any siblings?'

'No.'

Soon after that he pulled into the driveway of the cottage but he didn't kill the engine. Kellie knew he had probably regretted revealing as much as he had and was keen to get away before she got even further under his carefully guarded emotional radar.

'Thank you for the lift,' she said, opening the passenger door before he could stride around to do so.

'No trouble,' he said, not even looking her way. 'I'll send someone around tomorrow to fix that window for you. They're probably all a bit stiff. It's the heat at this time of year. It practically melts the paint.'

'Thanks,' she said with a little smile. 'I'd really appreciate it.'

She stood and watched as he drove away in a cloud of dust, the fine red particles his car stirred up making her eyes suddenly start to water.

Kellie spent a restless night in the cottage. The heat, in spite of the air-conditioning, was oppressive and there were noises throughout the night that had her senses constantly on high alert. First she thought she heard footsteps on the roof, but after she heard the distinctive territorial screech of a possum she settled down again.

A few minutes later she heard two cats spitting and yowling just outside her bedroom window. She got out of bed and, pulling aside the curtains, gritted her teeth as she opened the stiff window just enough to lean out and shoo the snarling cats away.

She was just about to close the window when she caught sight of a shadow moving stealthily across the neighbouring vacant property. Her blood stilled in her veins, her heart missed a beat, her throat closing over with fear as she saw the figure disappear into the scrub at the back of the block.

Sleep was almost impossible after that. The old house seemed to be full of squeaks and creaks; even the sound of the refrigerator intermittently regulating its thermostat was enough to have Kellie springing upright in bed each time in wide-eyed terror.

She hadn't realised living alone would be so...so...creepy.

What if someone was inside the house right now? What if they were not aware it was currently occupied and were on their way in? Kellie had heard of intruders reacting violently when confronted by the occupant of a residence they had assumed was vacant.

'I need to get myself a dog,' she said, not even realising she had spoken out loud until she heard the eerie echo of her voice in the stillness of the darkness.

The cats started up again outside her bedroom window and Kellie lay back on her pillow and began counting all the different breeds of dogs she could until through sheer exhaustion she finally drifted off to sleep...

CHAPTER SIX

THE morning sun was bright but without the sting of the day before so Kellie decided to use the cooler air to get in some exercise. Although the rolling ocean was her usual choice she was no stranger to jogging, and out here where the roads were seemingly endless and with little traffic she felt she could clear her head and prepare herself mentally for the months ahead.

She was well on her way when she realised it might have been a good idea to bring a water bottle with her and maybe even a map of the local area. She had taken a few left and then right turns on side roads to break the monotony of the long straight road but now she wasn't quite sure which way led back to town. The flat dry landscape all looked the same. An occasional gnarled gumtree offered a landmark now and again but as soon as she turned in another direction there was another one just like it.

The sun was beating down with increasing force and her mouth started to feel like she had been sucking on a gym sock for hours. The thought of something wet and cold was almost enough to make her begin to hallucinate. She even thought she could hear the rattle of ice cubes in a glass and the slight tang of a twist of lemon…

She bent down, her hands on her knees as she dragged in

a couple of dry, rasping breaths. Her brand-new running shoes were no longer pristine and white. Instead, they were stained with the ochre-coloured dust of the outback.

She gradually became aware of the sound of a motorbike on her left and she straightened to see a man approaching from behind a fenced property, where a herd of cattle was watching from the limited shade of a cluster of gumtrees, their wide eyes seeming—along with the motorbike rider and the kelpie riding on the back—to be seriously questioning her sanity.

Matt's first words confirmed her impression. 'What the hell are you doing this far out here without water?' he barked.

Kellie hated the ditsy, helpless female role. There was no way she was going to admit she had made a mistake, even if she knew she had indeed made one and a potentially life-threatening one at that. 'It's barely seven in the morning,' she said. 'I've only been running for half an hour or so.'

He frowned at her darkly. 'Then you must be an Olympic champion because you're at least nine kilometres from town. If you turn back now that will be a eighteen-kilometre round trip, which is just asking for muscle meltdown without adequate fluids in this sort of heat.'

Kellie narrowed her gaze to take in the acubra hat on his head. 'Well, now, Dr McNaught,' she said in a pert voice. 'Aren't you a fine one to be preaching health and safety issues with me when you're not wearing a helmet? You could have a fall off that bike of yours and end up concussed or brain injured.'

His jaw clenched slightly as his dark blue eyes tussled with hers. 'I'm on private property and driving at less than forty kilometres per hour.'

Kellie planted her hands on her hips and continued to stare him down. 'You could be driving at ten kilometres an hour and still come off and hit your head against a rock or something,' she pointed out.

He took off his hat and wiped his sweaty brow with the back of his hand. 'Yeah, well, it's too hot to wear one.'

'I'm afraid that excuse won't quite cut it with the cops if they pull you over on the road,' she countered, trying not to stare at the bulge of his biceps as his hands returned to grip the handlebars of the bike.

His eyes nailed hers. 'I don't ride my bike on the road.'

The dog, who up until this point had been perched—somewhat precariously in Kellie's opinion—on the back of the bike jumped off, and with an agility she could only envy wriggled on its belly underneath the fence and came over to nuzzle against her.

She bent down in delight and gave his velvet ears a gentle stroke, crooning to him softly. 'Well, hello, there, gorgeous boy. Have you been helping your daddy on the farm? What a good dog you are, and very clever too. I saw you balancing there like a gymnast on the back of that big bad old bike. Not many of the city dogs I know could do that.'

Matt felt like rolling his eyes but secretly he was a little impressed. Spike wasn't usually so good with strangers. He was a cautious dog, leaning a little towards the anxious if anything, but that was because he had been badly mistreated before Matt had rescued him from the dogs' home in Brisbane.

He watched as the dog melted under her touch, Spike's brown eyes turning to liquid as Kellie tickled him under the chin.

'Here, Spike,' he called, and whistled through his teeth.

Spike pricked his ears and looked at him, but then turned back to Kellie and rolled over in the dust, exposing his belly for a scratch.

'Oh you darling, *darling* boy,' Kellie gushed, scratching and stroking him simultaneously. 'You like that, huh? Yeah, well, I've never met a man yet who didn't like his stomach stroked, or his ego, too, for that matter. But you don't strike me as the overblown-ego type. You're a real sweetie, aren't you?'

Matt could feel his blood surging to places it hadn't surged to in years as he watched Kellie's hand move over his dog's exposed belly. But then the long length of her toned legs in those shorter-than-short running shorts was enough to set anyone's blood boiling, he thought. Her soft, sensual voice was like a whispery caress along the stiffness of his spine, and his deep abdominals switched on with a deep clench-like kick as he thought of how it would feel to have those slim, soft fingers skating over his naked flesh…

Kellie grinned as she straightened, the dog still nudging her hand with its head. 'He's so *cute*,' she said. 'I was just thinking last night how much I'd love to have a dog. Do you know anyone who's got one for sale?'

Matt hastily assembled his features into a stern frown. 'Dogs are not like toys to be picked up and played with at random. It takes commitment and patience to own and train one, especially a working dog. Besides, what would you want with a dog? You're only here for a few months. What will you do with it when you leave?'

She rolled her eyes at him. '*Duh!* I'll take it with me, of course,' she said. 'I love dogs. We've had dogs ever since I was a toddler. Our last one only died a few months ago. That was another reason I took this post. I couldn't bear to leave before Sadie lived her last days. I wanted to be there when she died.'

'And were you?'

Kellie couldn't quite read his expression due to the angle of the morning sun. 'Yes,' she said. 'I was the one who took her to the vet when I realised things were rapidly going downhill. When she was put down the vet left me alone with her and she died cradled in my arms. It was one of the most moving experiences of my life. It reminded me of my mother's death. It made me realise no one should ever die alone, not even the family pet.'

Matt looked at Spike, who was still licking Kellie's fingers as if they were coated in thick chocolate. 'If you want to share the space with Spike on the back, I'm willing to give you a lift back to the homestead and then on to town,' he said gruffly.

She raised her brows at him. *'On the bike?'*

'Only back to the homestead,' he clarified. 'After that you can have the assurance of airbags, stability control and ABS brakes all the way into town.'

'We-ll,' she said, shifting her lips from side to side as she considered his offer.

'I promise to drive extra-slowly,' he added.

'OK, then,' she said, and moved towards the fence with the dog at her side. 'Now, then, Spike, I'm not sure I'm going to do it your way. I think I'll go over the top.'

Matt propped his bike on its stand so he could offer his assistance but she had already snagged her jogging shorts on the top rung of barbed wire by the time he got there.

She looked down at him sheepishly, her perfect small white teeth sinking into her plump bottom lip. 'Oops,' she said, giving her shorts a little tug.

'Here,' he said, moving closer. 'Hold onto my shoulders and I'll unhitch you.'

Kellie put her hands on his shoulders, her belly giving a little quiver of reaction as she felt his hard muscular warmth seeping through the palms of her hands. Her fingers dug in a little further as she felt one of his hands releasing the fabric against her bottom and a shiver ran up like a startled mouse the entire length of her spine. Wow! Those hands of his sure had some magic about them, she thought as she hastily tried to disguise her reaction.

'There,' he said, his voice sounding a little scratchy. 'You're undone.'

'Th-thanks,' she said, locking gazes with him, her hands still on his shoulders.

The sounds of the bush seemed to Kellie to intensify the fact that apart from the dog and the herd of cattle they were not only totally alone but still physically touching.

Her fingers splayed experimentally, relishing the feel of toned male flesh, her belly doing another little flip-kick movement when she saw the dark unshaven stubble on his jaw. She suddenly wanted to run her fingers over the prickle of his skin, to feel it against the softness of hers, on her face, her mouth, her breasts and the silk of her inner thighs.

She looked back into his deep blue gaze and saw the unmistakable flare of male desire burning there. Her chest began to feel as if a moth was fluttering inside the soft cage of her lungs.

His hands went to her waist, the long fingers resting against her for perhaps a second or two longer than necessary before he lifted her from the fence. Kellie felt every angle and plane of his tall lean body on the way down, her breasts brushing against his pectoral muscles, her belly against the hard buckle of his belt, her trembling thighs against the rock-hard length and strength of his.

He set her on the ground and stepped back from her, his expression instantly shutting her out. 'Come on, then, hop on,' he said tonelessly, kicking the bike stand with his foot before straddling the bike.

Kellie had never realised how arrantly masculine such a simple action could be. 'Um…where's Spike going to sit?'

she asked, trying to sound calm and cool and totally unaffected when inside she felt every secret place pulsing with a need she had never felt in such strong, insistent waves before.

'He'll run alongside,' Matt said, and gave the dog a signal with one of his hands. 'It's not far and he'll enjoy the exercise.'

Kellie put one leg over the bike and moved as close to him as she dared, her inner thighs having to stretch to accommodate the muscular width of his. 'R-rightio,' she said a little uncertainly. 'I'm all set.'

He started the bike with a downward thrust of one booted foot. 'Put your arms around my waist,' he instructed. 'The ground's pretty rough in spots.'

'Er…right…' Kellie said, and nestled closer, her arms going around his trim taut middle, while her mind went to places she wasn't sure it should be going.

For instance, she knew if she inched her fingers just a teeny bit closer she could touch his male outline, the unmistakably *hard* male outline of him she had felt on her little sensual slide down his body. Or if she nudged herself even closer against his back, her feminine mound would be able to feel the tautness of his buttocks…

'Everything all right back there?' Matt asked after a journey of about fifty metres.

'Er…yes…fine…just fine…' she answered, wriggling back a bit.

Within a few minutes Kellie could see the homestead in the distance, the colonial design with its wrap-around veranda and large rainwater tanks an iconic image of rural life on the land.

The effects of the longstanding drought, however, were clearly visible. The gardens surrounding both residences looked worn down by thirst and the various trees offering what they could in terms of shade had a thick coat of red dust on their leaves.

Matt brought the bike to a standstill near one of the large sheds a short distance from the homestead and Kellie dismounted even before he had turned off the engine.

'How far behind will Spike be?' she asked.

'He'll probably stop for a quick dip in the home paddock dam,' he said, taking off his hat and brushing back his hair with his hand. 'And speaking of water, let's get you inside and rehydrated.'

Kellie followed him up the four well-worn steps to the front door, the cooler shade of the veranda an instant relief from the now fierce heat of the sun. Inside the house was even cooler, the long hallway with its polished timber floors and the smell of furniture polish and cedar making her feel as if she was stepping back in time to a previous era.

She looked around with interest as he led her to the kitchen. 'Wow, this is such a lovely house, Matt,' she said. 'It must be, what, a hundred and fifty years old?'

'Something like that,' he said, handing her a tall glass of water he had poured from a covered jug in the fridge.

Kellie felt the brush of his fingers as she took the glass and, averting her gaze, took a few sips even though she felt like throwing her head back and downing the contents in one gulping swallow.

'Help yourself to more water and feel free to make yourself tea or coffee,' he said as he headed to the door. 'Everything's there on the bench near the kettle. I'm just going to have a quick shower before we head into town.'

'Thanks,' she said and once he had left the room she quickly refilled her glass and drank deeply.

Kellie heard the sound of water being lapped thirstily

outside. She looked out of the window and was pleased to see Spike had made his way back and after his drink was making himself comfortable in the shade of the rainwater tank.

She wandered from the kitchen to the comfortable-looking sitting room across the hall, the sound of an ancient grandfather clock ticking yet again reminding her of how many generations of farmers had lived here.

Her gaze went to the mantel above the fireplace where there was a photograph of a young woman, the same woman she had caught a glimpse of in Matt's wallet the day before. She picked up the frame and looked into the features of his late fiancée, her long ash-blonde hair, almond-shaped green eyes and wide happy smile marking her as a stunningly beautiful woman.

The floorboards creaked as Matt stepped into the room and Kellie turned around, suddenly feeling like a child who had been caught with their hand in the cookie jar. 'I was just…um…having a look around,' she said, still holding the photograph.

He walked across the room, took the frame from her hands and looked down at it for an infinitesimal moment, before turning and carefully setting it back on the mantel in exactly the same position. Kellie got the impression he thought she had deliberately desecrated his shrine for his fiancée. She could see the tension in his shoulders as he stood with his back to her, still looking at the photograph.

'What was her name?' she found herself asking.

'Madeleine,' he answered after a slight pause.

'She was very beautiful,' Kellie said, not sure what else to say to fill the awkward silence.

'Yes…' He turned around to look at her, his expression showing none of the emotion she could hear in his voice. 'Yes, she was…'

The grandfather clock timed the next silence.

Kellie breathed in the clean scent of Matt, the tantalising combination of citrus-based shampoo and soap and aftershave activating all her senses. His dark brown hair was still wet, although it looked as if he had used his fingers rather than a comb to push it into place. His jaw was cleanly shaven now but it looked as if the razor had nicked him just below his chin on his neck. She could see the pinkish graze and she felt an almost uncontrollable urge to close the small distance between their bodies and salve the tiny wound with the tip of her tongue.

She ran her tongue over her parched lips instead, more than a little shocked at how she was reacting to him. She couldn't remember a time when she had felt so physically aware of a man. Her whole body was on high alert, her skin tingling to feel more of his touch. She could still feel the warm imprint of his hands where they had rested on her waist earlier, the nerve endings still fizzing like thousands of champagne bubbles under her skin.

'Matt, I was— Oh, sorry,' a gruff male voice said from the door. 'I didn't know you had company.'

'It's all right, Bob,' Matt said, turning to face the man. 'This is Kellie Thorne, the new GP filling in for Tim Montgomery. Kellie, this is Bob Gardner, my manager.'

Kellie smiled and took the older man's heavily calloused hand in hers. 'I'm very pleased to meet you, Bob,' she said with a bright and friendly smile.

'Nice to meet you, Dr Thorne,' Bob said. 'My wife Eunice would like to meet you some time. She's away at the moment, visiting our daughter in Cairns, but when she gets back I'm sure she'll invite you over for a meal or something.'

'I'll look forward to it,' Kellie said still smiling.

'What did you want to talk to me about, Bob?' Matt asked.

'That heifer we were worried about has delivered her twin calves without any dramas,' Bob said. 'But I thought we should still get a couple of antibiotic injections from Jim Webber just in case she comes down with milk fever.'

'Good idea,' Matt said. 'I'll drop in on my way home from the clinic, unless you're going to town.'

'I've got to see about that pump part so I can get them then,' Bob said. He turned again to Kellie and smiled. 'I hope you settle in quickly, Dr Thorne, and enjoy your time with us. Lord knows, Matt here could do with the back-up. He works too hard but that's life in the bush, I guess.'

'I'm looking forward to helping out in any way I can,' she said. 'In fact, the sooner the better.'

'Well…be seeing you,' Bob said, and, brushing off his hat, stepped out of the room.

Matt pushed back his partially dry hair with one hand. 'Wouldn't you like a couple more days to look around a bit first?' he asked. 'To settle in and find your way around?'

She shook her head, making her glossy chestnut ponytail swing from side to side. 'No, I've seen enough. I more or less know what I'm in for. I'm itching to get started.'

Matt felt a tiny wry smile lift one corner of his mouth. 'You really like diving into things boots and all, don't you?'

She gave him one of her high-wattage smiles in return. 'No point in living life unless you live it to the full, right?'

Matt had to force himself not to glance back at Madeleine perched on the mantel in her silver frame, but he felt her rainforest-green eyes watching him all the same. He had been promising himself he would put her away…well, not exactly in *that* sense. But he had come to realise recently there would always be a part of him that would think of Madeleine with deep affection. *What? Not love?* That tiny voice of conscience spoke inside his head, louder than it had in years.

Matt had thought he had loved Madeleine. They had been together for so long it was hard to say when the feelings he had assumed were love had started. As a young couple together for such a long time they had sort of gradually drifted into a deeper and deeper relationship. One thing had followed another and before he'd known it they'd been having an engagement party, and then a little while after that they had started planning a wedding…

He gave an inward grimace. Perhaps it was well and truly time to send Madeleine's photograph back to her parents. No doubt they would find a space for it among the unopened wedding presents and uncut wedding cake.

He gave himself a mental shake and reached for his keys. 'Let's get moving,' he said, and led the way out to his car.

CHAPTER SEVEN

THEY had barely travelled a kilometre or two on the way into town when Matt got a call on his mobile. Because he used his hands-free device to answer while he was driving, Kellie heard every word of the exchange.

'Matt, there's been an incident at Coolaroo Downs,' a female voice said. 'Apparently one of the jackaroos had some sort of altercation with a bull. I'm not sure how serious it is. You know what Joan Dennis is like these days—she panics if someone falls off a fence. It might be just a graze for all we know. The volunteer ambos are on their way but I thought you should see what gives before we call in the flying doctor.'

'Thanks, Trish,' Matt said. 'I'll head back that way now. I have the new GP with me but rather than drop her in to the clinic I think she'd better come with me just in case this is serious. Can you let the clinic patients know I might be half an hour or so late?'

'Sure,' Trish said. 'So…' An element of feminine intrigue entered her voice. 'What's she like?'

Matt tried to ignore the way Kellie's toffee-brown gaze turned towards him. He couldn't see it but he sure as hell could feel it. 'She's…er…with me right now,' he said.

'Yes, I know, that but what is she *like*?' Trish probed. 'Is she good-looking?'

'All right, I guess,' he said, wincing when he felt the laser burn of Kellie's look.

'All right as in what?' Trish kept on at him. 'As in girl-next-door or model material?'

Matt mentally rolled his eyes. 'Somewhere in between,' he answered, chancing a glance Kellie's way and then wishing he hadn't. Didn't he know enough about women to know they all wanted to be considered the most beautiful woman that ever walked the planet? Not that Kellie wasn't beautiful or anything. She was absolutely gorgeous now that he came to think about it. She had a natural elegance about her—in fact, he reckoned she'd look as fabulous in a slinky evening gown with full make-up and exotic perfume and glittering jewellery as she did in a ripped pair of running shorts with her hair limp with perspiration and her cheeks pink from exertion.

Ever since Matt had felt the slim slide of Kellie's body down his that morning out by the fence, he had been having some very disturbing and rather erotic thoughts about her. But he didn't like being manipulated and it seemed to him the whole town was conspiring to hook them up as a couple. When it came time for him to think about another relationship he would do it his way, the old-fashioned way, not because everyone felt sorry for him and had brought in their version of a mail-order bride.

Trish's voice cut through his private thoughts. 'So do you think you might ask her on a date or something?' she asked.

'Trish, I'm on hands-free here and Dr Thorne is hearing every word,' he said, wishing he'd thought to say it earlier, like about three sentences back.

'Oh… Well, then…' Trish quickly recovered and added, 'Hi, there, Dr Thorne. I'm Trish, the receptionist. We've been looking forward to having you join us.'

'I've been looking forward to being here, too,' Kellie said.

'In fact, so much so I'm prepared to get my hands dirty straight away. Dr McNaught has asked me to start a few days early.'

'Well, thank the Lord for that,' Trish said. 'We've been run off our feet while Matt was away on the weekend, and my husband David is supposed to be taking it easier these days. You're just what this place needs—a bit of new blood and young and single and female to boot.'

'Got to go, Trish,' Matt said curtly. 'Keep the phone line as free as you can until we see what gives.'

'Will do,' Trish promised, and promptly hung up.

Matt drove a few more kilometres down the seemingly endless road before he took a right turn into a property marked as Coolaroo Downs, the car rumbling over each of the cattle grids making Kellie rock from side to side in her seat.

He frowned as the cattle yards eventually came into view. 'This looks a little more serious than I thought,' he said. Glancing in the rear-view mirror, he added, 'I hope to God the ambulance isn't too far behind us.'

Kellie felt a tight knot of panic clutch at her insides as Matt parked the car a short distance from the small cluster of people hovering around the body of a young man lying on his back, a dark stain of blood spreading from his abdomen to the dusty ground beneath him.

Matt went round to the rear hatch to retrieve his emergency bag and drug pack. 'Here, take this,' he said, handing Kellie the drug pack, as they were met by Jack Dennis, the property owner.

'It's Brayden Harrison, our junior jackaroo,' Jack said, his face pale beneath his leathery tan. 'Didn't see our stud bull coming straight for him. When he turned, he got gored and thrown into the air. It's bad, Doc. I don't think he's going make it.'

From what Kellie could see, she thought Jack could be right, and sending a quick glance at Matt she could see he thought the same. Brayden was on his back, as white as a sheet and unconscious, hardly breathing. There was a large pool of dark blood still collecting by his side, coming from a wide slash in his abdomen, with a loop of bowel visible through the torn flannelette shirt.

Matt set his emergency pack down beside Brayden, and opened it out to reveal the colour-coded sections for trauma management. 'Jack, has the air ambulance been called?' he asked.

'Yes, Joan called them soon after she called you, but they told her they were on another call to Roma.'

'Have someone go up to the house and tell Joan to ask them to divert here now. There's every chance this is going to be a fatality unless we can pull off a miracle here,' Matt said. Turning to Kellie, he went on, 'He's in shock and unconscious. Put on gloves and goggles and come round to the side and stabilise his neck while I intubate him.'

Kellie held the neck steady, while Matt, now also with gloves and goggles on, gathered the laryngoscope and size 7 endotracheal tube. There was no suction, and the sun was bright, flooding out the light of the laryngoscope.

'Jack, hold this space-blanket over his head to make it darker so I can see down his throat,' Matt instructed with a calm confidence Kellie couldn't help admiring.

Under the cover of the blanket, Matt inserted the endotracheal tube, inflated the cuff and attached the respirator bag. There was no oxygen, only air to ventilate with.

'OK, I'll ventilate while you fit a hard cervical collar, Kellie. They're in the airway section,' Matt instructed.

Kellie retrieved and fitted the collar, then under Matt's instruction took over ventilation with the bag. Matt listened to the chest with his stethoscope, and then percussed the chest.

'There's very little air entry on the right and it's dull to percussion. I'd say he's got a haemothorax. He's also losing a lot of blood from the abdominal wound.'

Taking a pair of scissors, Matt cut away the front of the patient's shirt to reveal a ragged gash in the right upper quadrant of the abdomen, with a loop of bowel protruding and dark blood oozing out. Taking a pack of gauze dressings and a few ampoules of saline, Matt covered the bowel and compressed it back into the abdomen, then covered the whole wound with several large dressing packs and taped them down. He then inserted a 14-gauge cannula into a vein in the arm, and attached it to a litre bag of normal saline.

'Jack, here, squeeze this bag firmly to push the fluid in,' Matt directed, handing over the IV set to the cattle farmer.

One of the station hands came back down from the house to inform them, 'The flying doctor's diverting here. They should be overhead in about ten minutes.'

'Good,' Matt said, and inserted a second IV line into the other arm, and got the station hand to hold up the IV fluid bag.

Matt knew he had two more bags of saline in the kit which would hopefully be enough till help arrived. The flow of blood had now stopped, at least externally.

'OK, all we can do now is hold the fort and support his airway and circulation till we get more gear,' Matt said. 'I'll take over ventilation, Kellie. Can you do his obs?'

'Sure,' Kellie answered, becoming even more impressed at Matt's level-headedness under intense pressure and circumstances that were far from ideal. The dust and heat was bad enough but with the stickiness of blood the bush flies were starting to swarm around. 'Pulse is 120, BP 80 systolic,' she said. 'The first bag's through. I'll put up the next one.'

Seemingly from nowhere, the roar of a plane at low altitude

passed directly overhead, en route to the airstrip on the other side of the homestead.

'Thank God.' Matt breathed a sigh of relief. 'We might just pull this off yet.'

The final bag of saline was almost through when one of the station's four-wheel-drive vehicles arrived with the air ambulance crew in the back, together with a stretcher and several emergency kits. One of the ambulance crew jumped out, carrying two packs of equipment.

'Hi, I'm Marty Davis. We haven't got a doctor—he's in Roma with a placenta praevia. They've got things under control there but we're on our own here. What have you got?'

'Brayden Harrison, one of the jackaroos, has been gored by a bull and is in very bad shape,' Matt informed him. 'He's in haemorhagic shock, he's got a haemothorax and an open abdominal wound. Have you got any plasma expander? We've just exhausted our normal saline and we're still way behind.'

Kellie connected both of the bottles Marty produced to the IV lines while Matt instructed Marty and his partner, Helen, to position the stretcher beside the patient. While Kellie took over ventilation, Matt supervised the transfer onto the trolley and into the back of the four-wheel drive.

'He's still bleeding internally. I want to get him to the plane and put in a right intercostal catheter to re-expand his right lung. Have you got underwater drainage?' Matt asked.

'Yes, we've got a full set of stuff for chest wounds on the aircraft,' Helen said.

'Let's go, then,' Matt said. Exchanging a quick glance with Kellie, he asked, 'Are you OK to fly with me to Brisbane? I'll need you to ventilate him while I manage his IV fluids and abdominal wound.'

'Of course,' she said, although she could feel her stomach already beginning to tighten in apprehension.

Once they reached the aircraft, the two ambulance personnel loaded the patient, while Kellie and Matt set up the intercostal tray.

Kellie helped Matt wash his hands with some sterile water and surgical scrub solution.

'Thanks,' he said, locking gazes with her momentarily before he donned sterile gloves.

She watched as Matt prepped the right side of the chest before performing the necessary procedure that would stem the flow of blood. Some tense minutes later when he unclamped the tube, about 300 ml of blood drained into the bottle, with a small ongoing leak of blood after that.

'Hopefully his chest bleed will stop,' Matt said as he fixed the tube to the skin with a heavy suture and sticky plaster.

'You did an amazing job back there,' Kellie said, meeting his eyes across the now relatively stable patient. 'You stayed so calm and in control.'

Matt gave her a quick movement of his lips that could have almost passed for a smile. 'You were a damned good assistant,' he said. 'It makes a huge difference when everyone knows what to do and when to do it.'

'Thanks,' she said, feeling a blush spreading over her cheeks. 'But I was glad you were the one in charge.'

'I'm sure you would have coped just as well,' he said, checking the patient's condition again. 'Come on, Brayden, hold it together, mate. Not long now.'

Kellie heard the slight note of desperation in Matt's voice. 'Do you know him personally?' she asked softly.

His eyes connected with hers before looking away again to focus on the young man lying between them. 'I met him a few months ago. He came to see me about a plantar wart on his foot.' His frown deepened as he continued, 'He's nineteen years old. He was a little undecided about what to do after he finished school, so rather than waste his parents' money at university doing a course he might never use he came out to the bush for a gap year.' He let out a ragged sigh as his eyes came back to hers. 'He's just a kid…'

Kellie put her hand on his arm. 'He'll make it, Matt,' she said. 'You've done everything possible to get him this far. He *has* to make it.'

Matt looked down at her smooth hand resting against the dark tan of his skin. She had pretty fingers, long and slender with short but neat nails. The skin of her palm was soft and warm, and he found himself wondering what it would feel like to have her massage the aching tension out of his neck.

He pulled his hand away as if by doing so he could tug himself away from where his thoughts were wandering. It had been so long since he had felt a woman's touch. He had locked his physical needs away the day Madeleine had died. For six long lonely years he had ignored the natural and instinctive stirrings of his body, distracting himself with work until there hadn't been time or energy to think about what he was missing.

No one in all that time had made his skin lift and tighten simultaneously at the merest touch. No one's eyes had met his and seen more than he'd wanted them to see. No one's smile had melted or even chipped at the stone of sadness that weighed down his soul.

But Dr Kellie Thorne with her feather-light touch and brown eyes and beautiful smile certainly came close.

Perhaps a little too close.

CHAPTER EIGHT

ONCE the patient was transferred in Brisbane to the nearest trauma centre, Matt looked up at the flight information board and frowned. 'I hate to be the one to tell you this but it looks like we're going to have to cool our heels here for a while.'

Kellie looked up at the screen. 'Why?'

Brian King, the pilot who had flown the patient down, came over to where they were standing. 'There are electrical storms all over the region,' he explained. 'Most of the regional flights have been grounded overnight.'

'*Overnight?*' Kellie blinked a couple of times. 'But I've got nothing with me. Look at me.'

Both men turned and looked at her.

Kellie felt her face go red when Matt's dark blue gaze lingered the longest. 'I'm covered in blood and dust,' she said, and added mentally, *And I'm wearing a pair of ripped high-cut running shorts and a vest top, and I haven't had a shower and I've never felt so unfeminine and unattractive in my life.* 'Anyway, where would we stay?' she asked.

'There's a hotel close to the airport we use at times like this,' Brian said. 'They do a cheap rate for medical personnel. I'd offer you a bed at my place but we're in the middle of renovations. There's barely room for the wife and kids.' He turned to Matt. 'Will you stay at your…er…fiancée's parents'?'

'No,' Matt said, his expression as blank as a bare wall. 'They've got relatives staying with them this week. I'll be fine at the hotel with Dr Thorne.'

'I reckon the flights will be back to normal in the morning,' Brian said. 'Are you guys right to get a taxi? I've got to go through a couple of checks with the safety crew.'

'Sure,' Matt said. Giving Kellie a follow-me nod, he led the way outside to the taxi rank.

Kellie could feel every person's eyes on her as she stood beside Matt in the queue. An older couple in front had even made a point of stepping away from her, their wrinkled brows frowning in disapproval as they'd taken in her dishevelled appearance.

She felt Matt's broad shoulder brush against her. 'Ignore them,' he said in a low voice.

She looked up at him and asked in an undertone, 'Do I smell?'

His expression contained a hint of wryness. 'I've smelt worse.'

'Thanks,' she said, rolling her eyes. 'That's very reassuring.'

A flicker of a smile lit his gaze. 'Believe me, you'll feel like a million dollars after a shower and something to eat,' he said, as he led her to the next available taxi.

It was a short trip to the hotel, where the receptionist at the front desk smiled apologetically at Matt's request for two rooms. 'I'm terribly sorry, sir, but we only have one room available.'

Matt frowned. 'One room?'

'I'm afraid so,' she answered. 'With so many regional flights being cancelled at short notice, we filled up very quickly.'

'I don't mind sharing a room,' Kellie piped up helpfully.

Matt's frown brought his brows almost together as he looked down at her for a moment.

'It's only for one night,' she said, conscious of the receptionist's speculative look.

'It's a queen-sized suite,' the receptionist chipped in. 'But if you would like a roll-out bed brought in I can organise Housekeeping to have one delivered to your room.'

'Yes,' Matt said. 'That would be very much appreciated.'

'We're not a couple,' Kellie explained.

'Brother and sister?' The receptionist took a wild guess.

'No,' Kellie said with a little laugh. 'I've already got five brothers. The last thing I need is another one.'

The receptionist smiled as she handed Matt a form to sign. 'It's room four hundred and twenty-five,' she said. 'You'll need your swipe card. I hope you enjoy your stay.'

When the doors of the first available lift opened Kellie stared in dismay at her reflection in the mirrored wall at the back. 'Oh, my God!' she wailed. 'Why didn't you tell me I looked like this?'

Matt reached past her to press the button for their floor. 'You don't look that bad,' he said with what he hoped was an indifferent look.

She groaned as she rubbed at the smear of blood over her right cheek with the bottom of her top. 'I look like an extra from a horror movie,' she said. 'The least you could have done is said something. No wonder people were staring.'

'Yes, well, they probably weren't staring at your face,' Matt said dryly, doing his level best not to stare at the strip of tanned and toned abdomen she had exposed by lifting her top to clean her face.

She let the top fall back down. 'What do you mean?'

He put an arm out to hold the lift doors open. 'I think that rip in your shorts is getting bigger,' he said. 'I hope for the sake of your dignity there's a complimentary sewing kit in the room.'

Kellie clutched at her behind and felt the lace of her knickers. 'Oh, no!'

'Don't worry,' he said, leading the way down the hall. 'There's no one about. This is our room right here.'

Our room.

Matt felt himself flinch as he said the words. Those words… How many times had he and Madeleine used them over the years? Our first date, our love, our engagement, our future…

He stared at the swipe key in his hand, wondering if he should have tried another hotel. Why hadn't he thought of it earlier? It wasn't as if the whole of Brisbane would have been booked out. There were numerous hotels all over the city and even if some of them were beyond the health department budget, he could have paid for a couple of rooms himself.

'Hurry up!' Kellie said at his side. 'Open the door. I don't want anyone else to see like me this.'

He drew in a breath and opened the door, but before he could reach for the light switch she had rushed past him and headed straight to the bathroom.

While she was in the shower someone from Housekeeping arrived with a roll-out bed, which, once it was set up, shrank the space to give the room an alarmingly intimate feel.

Matt swung away and looked out of the window, trying not to think of Kellie's naked body standing under the shower next door. His whole body felt tense, his blood surging to his groin at the thought of spending the night in the same room as her with less than a metre of space to separate them. He was angry at himself, angry that he was allowing sheer animal attraction to override his common sense.

He closed his eyes and tried to think of Madeleine, but her

features seemed less defined, blurry almost, as if she was slowly but inexorably moving out of focus. He clenched his fists and tried to recall the scent of her perfume but even that, too, had drifted out of his reach.

'I'm all done,' Kellie said as she came out of the bathroom.

Matt slowly turned from the window, his lower belly kicking in reaction at the sight of her in one of the hotel's fluffy white bathrobes, her wet hair loose about her shoulders, the fresh orange-blossom fragrance of the shampoo and shower gel she had used filling his nostrils.

'I've washed out my things and left them to dry over the shower screen,' she said. 'I hope they won't be in your way while you shower.'

'Right...' he said, moving past her. 'Er...do you want to have a look through the room-service menu? It takes them about forty minutes to deliver it. You can order for me.'

'What would you like?' she asked.

Matt wasn't sure he could even admit that to himself without another pang of shame slicing through him. 'Anything,' he said. 'Surprise me.'

Kellie frowned as the bathroom door closed and locked behind him. After a moment or two she let out a little sigh, reached for the room-service menu and started reading.

Matt told himself he wasn't even going to look at the tiny pair of black lace knickers hanging over the glass shower screen, but as he blindly reached for the bath gel they fell off and landed at his feet. He waited a beat or two before bending to pick them up, his fingers almost of their own accord squeezing the moisture out of them.

He hung them back up with careful precision and quickly finished his shower, but somehow the thought of Kellie standing where he was standing just minutes before, the water coursing over and caressing her slim form, unsettled him far more than he wanted to admit.

She was sitting with her legs curled underneath her on the roll-out bed, reading a tourist brochure, when he finally came out of the bathroom. She looked up and smiled at him in that totally engaging way of hers and informed him, 'I've ordered you a steak with kipler potatoes and green vegetables. Is that OK?'

His stomach grumbled in anticipation. 'That's perfect,' he said as he rubbed his wet hair with his towel. 'What are you having?'

'I couldn't decide between the barramundi fillets with mango chilli salsa or the chicken with pesto and pine-nut stuffing or the loin of lamb with rosemary and garlic.'

He tried not to stare at the soft plumpness of her mouth. 'So…what did you decide?' he asked.

She tilted her head at him. 'What do *you* think I chose?'

'The fish,' he said, feeling an involuntary smile pull at the corners of his mouth. 'Definitely the fish.'

Her eyes went wide with surprise. 'How on earth did you guess that?'

He gave his head another quick rub with the towel. 'You're a beach chick,' he said. 'You've probably grown up with fish bones between your teeth.'

She grinned at him. 'I did, too,' she said. 'My brothers and I were taught to fish when we were still in nappies. I think I still hold the record for the most flathead caught in one outing.'

Matt marvelled yet again at how different their family backgrounds were. His father had taken him fishing once but it had been a disaster from start to finish. If the rain hadn't been bad enough, the seasickness Matt had felt on the way home across the bay had made it a day to remember for all the wrong reasons. He could still recall his father's scowling expression, as if Matt had been personally responsible for both the lack of fish and the inclement weather.

'You sound like you had a very happy childhood,' he said as he tossed his towel over the back of a chair.

'I did,' she said with another little smile. 'I hope when I get married and have kids, I'll be able to give them the sort of childhood I had.'

A stretching silence made the room seem ever smaller.

'I'm sorry....' Kellie said, biting her lip. 'I guess that was a bit insensitive of me.'

He gave her an unreadable look. 'No, not at all.'

Another beat or two of silence passed.

'Tell me about her,' Kellie said softly.

'Tell you about who?'

'Madeleine. Your fiancée. What was she like?'

Matt felt his chest start to tighten but after a moment's hesitation he found himself telling her more than he had told anyone. 'She was beautiful, a bit on the shy side but when she got to know you she would come out of her shell a bit more. She was an only child like me so we had a lot in common right from the start. We both found it hard to make friends easily. It took us time to learn to trust people.'

He took in a breath and continued, 'She loved music, not that techno modern stuff but mostly classical. She played the piano and the flute like a pro but she couldn't cook for peanuts.' He gave a ghost of a smile that barely touched his mouth and went on, 'I think it was because her mother and father did everything for her. Being their only child, it was understandable she was treated like a princess.'

'Her parents must miss her dreadfully,' Kellie said into the small silence.

His eyes met hers. 'Yes...' He released a long, rough-around-the-edges sigh. 'She was their life, their entire focus for living. They're like empty shells now.'

Kellie moistened her dry lips. 'It's nice that you keep in contact with them,' she said. 'Not many men in your situation would think to do that.'

He gave a rueful twist of his mouth but it wasn't anywhere near a smile. 'I'm not sure if it helps or hinders them, to tell you the truth,' he confessed. 'If I don't call them regularly I feel guilty, but when I do call it sort of stirs it all up again for them, you know?'

She nodded. 'I do know…'

He ran a hand through his still damp hair and sighed again. 'It's been six years and yet it sometimes feels as if it was yesterday.'

'What happened?' Kellie asked.

He sat on the end of the queen-sized bed, his legs so close that Kellie knew if she uncurled hers from beneath her they would touch his, knee to knee.

She watched the pain of remembering moving like a shadow over his face. It thinned his mouth, it tightened his jaw and it left his dark blue gaze achingly empty as it connected with hers.

'We had an argument the night before,' he said, a frown bringing his brows almost together over his eyes. 'I don't even remember what it was about now, something silly to do with the wedding seating arrangements, I think. She left in a huff and I was my usual pigheaded self, brooding over it for hours without doing anything to sort things out.'

Kellie sat in silence, somehow sensing he was letting his guard down in a way he had never done before. It made her feel an intimate connection with him, unlike anything she had felt with anyone else in the past.

His mouth contorted again as he continued, 'She was

spending the week with her parents so I didn't bother ringing her the next morning. I planned to go round that evening with flowers and an apology but, of course, I was too late. A car ran a red light and ploughed straight into her on her way to school that morning. She died a few minutes later at the scene.'

'I'm so sorry,' Kellie said in a voice whisper soft.

He brought his gaze back to hers, the bleakness of it making her ache for him. 'I often lie awake at night and wonder what she was thinking in those final moments as her life ebbed away,' he said. 'I wonder if she was thinking about me, our wedding and all the plans we'd made.'

Kellie brushed at her eyes. 'It must have been an absolute nightmare for you. I don't know how you coped.'

He gave her a crooked smile but it was grim, not humorous. 'It felt like a nightmare at the time,' he said. 'I kept thinking surely someone's going to tap me on the shoulder and say "April Fool" or something, but each day was the same as the one before. The grief was like a thick fog, I couldn't see through it and no one could get to me through its black heavy shroud. I even thought about…you know…ending it all.'

'What stopped you?'

His gaze meshed with hers. 'See these?' he asked, holding out his hands palms upwards.

Kellie nodded.

He looked down at his outstretched hands. 'These hands have been trained to save lives. I gave up years of my life to train to be a doctor. I had to work harder than most as I didn't have the support of my parents, who were too busy feuding with each other to take much notice of me. I thought it would be selfish of me to end it all when I could put my life to much better use.'

'So you came out to the bush.'

His eyes came back to hers. 'Yes. Out here I can make a difference. My life counts for something, even though it is not the life I had originally planned for myself.'

Kellie leaned forward and took his hands in hers and gently squeezed. 'You are an absolutely *amazing* doctor, Matt,' she said. 'You saved Brayden Harrison's life today.'

'He's not out of the woods yet,' he reminded her, but Kellie couldn't help noticing he didn't pull out of her tender hold.

'Perhaps not,' she said. 'But he's in with a chance, a chance he wouldn't have had if you hadn't been there to do what needed to be done.'

His fingers curled around hers, his slightly rough touch against her smooth one sending her pulse skyrocketing. She ran her tongue over her lips again, mesmerised by the dark intensity of his gaze as it held hers.

The doorbell of the suite sounded, announcing the arrival of their meals, and broke the moment. Matt dropped her hands as if they were hot coals and strode over to the answer the door.

The trolley was wheeled in and Matt gave the young attendant a tip on his way out before coming back to where Kellie was still curled up on the makeshift bed.

'We should eat this before it gets cold,' he said, without meeting her gaze.

Kellie knew he was regretting his earlier outburst of guilt and grief. She had experienced it so many times with her brothers, the way they let their guard down and then pulled away from her as if they were worried she would exploit their brief vulnerability. 'Matt?' she said softly.

He took the lid off one of the plates. 'This is your fish,' he said, and handed it to her with a closed-off expression.

'Don't shut me out,' she said, ignoring the outstretched

plate. 'Come on, Matt, you just let me into your deepest pain and now you're shoving me away.'

He blew out a breath and slapped the plate back down on the trolley. 'Don't eat it, then, see if I give a damn.'

She got to her feet and tugged at his arm. 'Matt, look at me,' she said. 'Stop feeling sorry for yourself. You can't bring her back no matter how much you want to. It wasn't your fault she died. You weren't to blame.'

He brushed off her arm, his eyes blazing as they hit hers. 'What would you know?' he barked at her savagely. 'What the hell would you know about how I feel?'

'I know more than you realise,' she said with quiet dignity. 'I know that you feel somehow responsible for Madeleine's death. I also know you are punishing yourself as if in some way that will make things right, but it won't, Matt. You won't make things right by doing wrong things.'

'What wrong things am I doing?' he asked, still glaring at her heatedly.

She came over to where he was standing, so close he had no where to go but back up against the wall. 'You didn't die in that accident with her, Matt,' she said. 'You're still alive and entitled to live a fulfilling life. You have the right to enjoy what life has to offer, you don't have to be a hermit out there in the bush. You can have a new love, maybe even a happy future, with marriage and babies.'

His lip curled in a sneer. 'Is that why you came out here?' he asked, 'to find a husband and sperm donor?'

Kellie flinched away from his crude bitterness. 'I came out here because I needed a change of scene. My family has become too dependent on me and my love life totally sucks, so all round it seemed like a good solution.'

He moved past her to lift the lid off the other plate. 'I'm

not interested in auditioning for the role of fill-in partner while you sort out your relationship and family issues. When I feel ready to look for another relationship I will do so in my own good time and not a minute before.'

'Only because you're afraid of being hurt again,' she said. 'It's understandable. My father is the same but it doesn't mean either of you don't deserve to live life to its fullest potential. You are, what, thirty-three or -four? You have more than half your life ahead of you. What are you doing, locking yourself away from all that life has to offer?'

He picked up the napkin-wrapped cutlery and sat on the bed with his plate balanced on his lap. 'I'm happy with my life the way it is. I work, I eat and I sleep.'

Kellie gave her eyes a roll of exasperation. 'Yes, but you do it all alone.'

'Only the sleeping part,' he said, sticking his fork into a floret of broccoli and popping it into his mouth.

Her eyes widened. 'You've been celibate for *six* years?'

Matt frowned at her. 'What's wrong with that?' he asked. 'Lots of people choose to be celibate.'

'I know but don't you think it's time you lived a little?'

'I told you, Kellie, I like my life the way it is for the moment,' he said. 'I'm sorry if Trish and the Montgomerys gave you the impression I was a likely candidate for a six-month fling but I prefer to choose my own partners, not have them thrust on me.'

Kellie glared at him. 'You think I would agree to a match-making scheme like that?' she asked. 'Get real, Matt. I like to choose my own partners too, not that I've been particularly good at it or anything, but don't for a moment think I would consider *you* as a potential lover, far from it.'

He pushed his half-eaten meal to one side and got to his

feet. 'I'm going out for some fresh air,' he said, tossing his napkin down on the bed. 'Don't wait up.'

Kellie blew out a frustrated sigh and pushed her half-eaten meal away. OK, so maybe that had been a bit harsh, she thought. The truth was she had more than once considered Matt as a potential lover, but after Harley's brazen two-timing Kellie was damned if she was going to play second fiddle to another woman again: dead or alive.

CHAPTER NINE

WHEN Matt came back to the suite at close to two a.m. Kellie was sound asleep, her small body curled up like a child's, one of her hands underneath her cheek, the other hanging down over the side of the bed.

He stood looking at her in the lamplight, feeling guilty for drinking in the sight of her while she was totally unaware of his presence. It seemed voyeuristic, exploitative even, but he couldn't seem to pull his gaze away.

She had obviously dispensed with the bathrobe for it was now hanging off the edge of the bed near her feet. Somehow the thought of her naked beneath that thin cotton sheet stirred his senses more than he would have thought possible. She had such a neat body, lean and athletic but unmistakably feminine.

He went rigid when she suddenly rolled over with a little murmur, the sheet slipping to reveal the creamy curve of one small but perfect breast. He knew he shouldn't be staring— he was a doctor, for pity's sake! He'd seen more breasts than he could count, and yet the sight of that creamy globe with its dusky brown nipple took his breath away.

Her soft mouth opened slightly on a sigh and she nestled back down into the pillow, but just when Matt thought it was safe to draw in a breath she suddenly opened her eyes. She sat bolt upright, her mad scramble for the sheet to cover herself affording him an even better view of her body than she had probably intended.

'What the hell do you think you're doing?' she railed at him. 'You scared me half to death!'

'Sorry,' he mumbled gruffly. 'I didn't mean to wake you. I was just…'

'You were just what?' She glared at him. 'Having a little peek while you thought no one was looking?'

He raked a hand that wasn't quite steady through his hair. 'It wasn't like that at all,' he lied, a tide of colour heating the back of his neck. 'I was trying to get to my bed without disturbing you in the process.'

'How long have you been standing there?'

His eyes shifted away from her accusing narrowed ones. 'Not long.'

'How long?'

'Can we, please, drop this?' he asked. 'Look, I have no designs on you so you can rest easy.'

She hugged her knees under the sheet, her expression looking a little downbeat. 'So…what you're saying is you don't find me in the least bit attractive?'

Matt frowned at the edge of insecurity in her tone. 'Of course I find you attractive,' he said. 'You're very attractive—gorgeous, in fact. Why on earth would you think otherwise?'

She gave her bottom lip a bit of a nibble before she answered. 'I don't know… I guess I'm not all that confident on the dating scene. I think I spent too much time sweating over making dinner for my father and my brothers instead of getting hot and sweaty in a nightclub with the rest of my friends. I keep thinking there must be something wrong with me. My ex certainly made it clear I wasn't enough to hold his interest.'

'Yeah, well, if you ask me, your ex was a jerk,' Matt said, pulling down the covers on the queen-sized bed in case he was tempted to cross the floor and pull her into his arms and show her how achingly beautiful she was.

A little silence passed.

'If the tables had been turned, would you have expected Madeleine to put her life on hold indefinitely?' Kellie asked.

'Look, Kellie,' he said injecting his tone with impatience at her persistence over his lack of a love life. 'I'm not putting my life on hold. But even if I was, it's not the same thing. It's so much harder for women.'

'How?' Kellie asked. 'Grief is grief. I don't think either gender has an exclusive take on it.'

'The issue of fertility puts a very definite take on it,' he pointed out. 'As a man, if I chose to I can have children at almost any age. Of course, in my twenties, thirties or forties would be ideal, but for women that isn't the case. They have limited time in which to select a suitable partner to father their child or children.'

'Did you and Madeleine plan to have children?'

Matt turned from the bed to look at her. 'It was something we discussed once or twice.' He looked away again, not comfortable adding how often he had shied away from the topic. Madeleine had been a few more steps ahead of him, now that he thought about it. It had been her idea to get engaged, her idea to bring the wedding forward and very definitely her idea to begin a family straight afterwards. It wasn't that Madeleine wouldn't have made a great mother, it was just he had never really seen himself settling down into suburbia in quite the way she had planned. It was a disturbing realisation that two people who had claimed to be in love had not really been in tune with each other's wants and desires. Was that why he was still punishing himself? he wondered. It wasn't that he had loved Madeleine too much—it was more that he hadn't loved her enough…

Kellie lay back on her pillow with her hands propped behind her head. 'My mother would have loved to be a grandmother,' she said on the end of little sigh. 'She told me that being a mother was great but it was so exhausting she couldn't wait to be a granny so she could hand back the little ones at the end of the day. I feel sad she won't be around for my babies, to love and indulge them as a doting granny should. My dad will do his best but it won't be the same, will it?'

Matt sat on the edge of his bed. 'I'm sure he will do what he can to be a good grandfather,' he said, rather unhelpfully.

She turned her head to look at him, a soft smile curving her mouth. 'I'm hoping my time away in the bush will bring about a romance.'

He automatically tensed. 'So I was right about Tim and Claire?' he said, clenching his jaw. 'I knew it. I just knew they wouldn't be able to help themselves.'

She gave him a blank look. 'What have Tim and Claire got to do with my father and my aunt?'

It was Matt's turn to deliver the blank stare. 'Your father and your aunt?'

'Yes,' Kellie said. 'My aunt has been in love with my father for the last five years, ever since she watched him nurse my mother through her illness. Aunty Kate's husband left her for another woman years ago, and for as long as I can remember she has always been there for all of us, working tirelessly in the background, dropping in meals or doing loads of washing and ironing without being asked. My father has more or less been oblivious to it because I've been there to pick up where she left off. I thought it would be best if I moved out so she

could show Dad how much she does for us and for him. He's a bit on the slow side, if you know what I mean.'

'He's probably not quite ready to move on,' he said pragmatically. 'You can't force him.'

'I know, but Aunty Kate loves him,' she said. 'She's loved him for years. I've known it, my brothers have known it even though they are about as emotionally deficient as boys can be, but my father seems completely ignorant of it.'

'Then perhaps it was a good move of yours to come out to the bush,' he said. 'You sound to me like the glue that holds your family together.'

'I'd never thought of it quite like that. That's great way to put it.' Her smile faded a little as she asked, 'But what if they fall apart while I'm gone?'

'I'm sure they won't,' Matt said. 'They've probably got into a pattern of learned helplessness. They'll soon snap out of it.'

'Yes, well, that's the plan,' she said with another little smile.

Matt could see that Kellie was a warm-hearted person who had a mission in life to spread love and goodwill to others. He also knew from what she had briefly intimated that her love life was lacking something, but it didn't mean he was the person to step up to the plate to take the next ball, certainly not with the whole of Culwulla Creek on the sidelines, cheering him on.

Anyway, life was *so* damned capricious.

Doctors knew that more than most. They diagnosed terminal illnesses on a weekly, sometimes even daily basis. He had done it himself. So many faces drifted past him, shocked faces, devastated faces, faces that communicated their frustration in their but-I've-not-done-all-I've-set-out-to-do expressions of despair.

They were all the same, just like him: cheated of what life had promised but had failed to deliver.

Was it his fault?

No, and the rational part of him knew Madeleine's death wasn't really his fault. It was the driver running the red light, it was the rush hour, it was a hundred other things that had been going on in the universe at that particular moment, but yet still he felt somehow responsible. What if she had been thinking about *him* at that moment and not seen the car on her right? What if she had been thinking about the seemingly endless list of jobs to do before their wedding? Or, like him, having last-minute doubts? It had been a stressful time, especially as Madeleine hadn't wanted to take any time off school and therefore everything had had to be packed into those last couple of days before the term finished. What if *he* had done more of those little jobs for her so she hadn't been so rushed off her feet?

The what-ifs had been what had kept him awake most nights in those early days and tortured far too many of his days as well. Work out here in the bush was his only panacea and so far it had done a reasonable job…well, it had until Kellie had come to town with her big smile and adorable dimples.

'We'd better get some sleep,' he said, feigning a yawn. 'The first flight is at eight. I organised it when I went out earlier. We were lucky as there were only two seats left.'

'I hope I get the window one,' she said, turning on her side and propping herself on her elbow.

Matt decided it would be wise to turn out the lamp as soon as he could so he didn't have to keep staring into those beautiful brown eyes. The soft light in the room made her gaze melting and soft, so soft he could feel himself drowning in it every time she looked at him. He muttered something about using the bathroom and came out a few minutes later dressed in the other bathrobe provided by the hotel. She was still

lying facing him, her eyes widening slightly when he got between the covers without taking off the bathrobe.

'You're going to cook, wearing that to bed,' she informed him knowledgably. 'I had to toss mine off hours ago.'

I wish you hadn't reminded me of that, Matt thought as he turned off the lamp and flopped down on the pillow. The thought of her satin skin covered only by the thin threads of a cotton sheet was almost too much for his mind to cope with.

There was barely a beat of silence before her voice split the silence.

'Matt?'

He affected a bored, I'm-almost-asleep tone. 'Hmm?'

'Do you think you could leave the lamp on?' she asked in a beseeching whisper.

Even though his eyes were closed Matt still rolled them behind his eyelids. 'What on earth for? Do you want to read or something? It's close to three in the morning.'

'No but it's so dark in here…'

He thumped the pillow to reshape it. 'It's supposed to be dark,' he said dryly. 'It's the middle of the night.'

'Yes, but I like to be able to see my way to the bathroom,' she said. 'I don't want to break a leg or something, stumbling in the dark.'

'Do you need the bathroom?'

'Not right now, but I might later.'

Matt removed his bathrobe under the cloak of darkness and placed it over the nearest chair before switching on the bedside lamp, turning the dimmer switch as low as it could go. 'There, it's on now so close your eyes and go to sleep.'

There was another beat or two of silence.

'Matt?'

He inwardly groaned. 'Yes?'

'Have you ever wondered what it would be like to be totally blind?' she asked.

He counted to five. 'Not lately, no.'

He heard the rustle of the bedclothes as she shifted her position. 'I do, a lot,' she said. 'I had a young female patient who was blind from retinoblastoma. She had lost both eyes by the time she was two years old. She told me what it was like, how she has to read people not by their faces or body language but by using other senses. She has to memorise every place she visits. No one can move a single piece of furniture at her house otherwise she'll bump into it. I think about it a lot—you know how you would have to adjust in so many little ways.'

'Do we have to talk about this now?' he asked, smothering a weary yawn, not a feigned one this time.

'No, it's just ever since I met her I feel like I have to have light around me,' she said. 'It reminds me of what so many people, me included, take for granted.'

'You do realise you are contributing unnecessarily to global warming?' he asked.

Kellie turned to look at him. He had dispensed with the bathrobe and was now lying on his back with his eyes closed, his arms propped behind his head, his biceps bulging, and his stomach flat and naked to his waist where the thin cotton sheet was resting. His chest was as tanned as the rest of his body, not entirely hairless but not overly so. The trail of black curly hair burrowed below the sheet to where it loosely covered his groin.

Kellie knew she shouldn't be staring but it had been a very long time since she had seen a man in such fabulous physical condition. Her pulse fluttered like a trapped moth beneath her skin.

She was less than a metre away from him. She could reach

out with one of her hands and slide it down his ridged abdomen; her fingers could splay over his maleness, stirring it to fervent life with the merest brush of her fingertips.

'It'd be tough, though, don't you think?' she asked, forcing her mind away from the temptation of his body. 'Being blind, I mean.'

Matt opened his eyes and turned to look at her and then wished he hadn't. The shadow of her cleavage was right in his line of vision and the delicious curves of her breasts were outlined by the sheet tucked against her. Even if he closed his eyes again he knew it would be impossible to erase that vision from his mind.

Possibly for ever.

'Aren't you exhausted?' he said. 'You've had a tough day, by anyone's standards.'

She wriggled under the bedclothes again and let out a tiny sigh. 'I guess I am a *bit* tired…'

Thank God, Matt thought as he watched her eyelids start to droop. He watched as she drifted off, her mouth relaxing into a soft plump curve, her slim form covered by the sheet making him wish he could run his hand over her, exploring every dip and curve of her body.

He clenched his hands into fists, scrunching his eyes shut, but the gentle sound of her breathing kept him awake for most of the night.

Bright morning sunlight pierced Kellie's eyelids and she sat bolt upright and rubbed at her eyes. 'Hey,' she said, glancing at her watch. 'Aren't we supposed to have left by now?'

Matt dragged his head off the pillow and looked at the bedside clock through slitted eyes. He muttered a stiff curse and threw off the bedclothes without thinking.

He suddenly saw Kellie's eyes go wide and then the delicate rise of colour rush up over her face. He reached for the bathrobe he'd discarded the night before and, tying it with more haste than security, lunged for the phone.

Kellie overheard every word of the exchange, realising as the heated conversation went on they would have to hurry or they would miss the only flight to Culwulla Creek that day, which would mean a long road trip in a hire car from Brisbane.

Using the sheet as a cover, she scuttled into the bathroom and tried not to think about what she had seen in that brief lapse when he had leapt from the bed, although she knew it was going to be very hard to erase it from her mind.

Matt was built like a bodybuilder, not the over-the-top anabolic steroids type but the type that sent female pulses soaring. Pumped muscles, leanness where leanness looked best, like on the flat planes of a stomach that looked as if it had been carved from a slab of marble.

When she came out dressed in her rinsed-out shorts and top and running shoes he was dressed and ready to go. 'We have to hurry,' he said, scooping up his doctor's bag. 'They're holding the flight for us but only because we're medical personnel.'

The attendant smiled at Matt as he led the way up the gangway. 'Well done, Dr McNaught,' she said, 'and with three minutes to spare.'

Matt gave her a brief smile in return and, nodding in apology to the already seated and belted passengers, indicated for Kellie to precede him. 'You can have the window seat,' he said with a deadpan expression. 'And the armrest too, if you want it.'

Kellie grinned up at him as she wriggled into the seat. 'Is that a sense of humour I see peeking out from behind that gruff exterior of yours?' she asked.

His expression remained bland but she saw his lips twitch slightly as he took his seat and began rummaging for his end of the seat belt.

'Is this what you're looking for?' she asked, holding up the clip-in end of the belt, her eyes twinkling mischievously.

Matt took it from her slim warm fingers, his body tingling all over at that merest of touches. She was smiling at him in that impish way of hers, the mixture of tomboy and sexy siren that befuddled his brain and other parts of his anatomy. He could feel the way his groin was already tightening, the ache building even more when she ran her tongue over the pink sheen of her lips in that slightly nervous, uncertain manner of hers. He thought of that soft mouth exploring him, the tip of her tongue tasting the essence of him, licking from him the life force that was banked up inside him to the point of bursting. All night he had thought of her hands skating over him, discovering his contours, feeling the length and deep throbbing pulse of him in the slim sheath of her body, the feminine heart of her convulsing around him as he drove himself to paradise…

Kellie peered at him curiously. 'Are you all right, Matt?' she asked.

Matt gave himself a mental shake and resettled in his seat, wincing as he had to accommodate a little more of himself than normal. 'I'm fine,' he muttered. 'These seats are so damned uncomfortable. There's not enough leg room.'

'That's because you're so tall,' she said, pushing his elbow off the armrest and smiling at him playfully.

Matt reached for the in-flight magazine in the seat pocket, even though he'd read it a thousand times before. Those long legs of hers were still in his line of vision. He couldn't help imagining them looped around his, her mouth on his, her tongue mating with his as they strove for mutual fulfilment.

He felt her shoulder lean into him. 'Interesting article?' she asked.

He schooled his features into impassivity as he looked at her. 'Absolutely riveting,' he said, and turned back to the piece on emu-oil investment.

CHAPTER TEN

RUTH WILLIAMS was at the airstrip when they alighted from the plane. 'I organised one of Jack Dennis's boys to take your car to the clinic,' she said to Matt. 'I didn't want to leave it out here overnight, especially with your medical equipment on board. I can give you a lift back into town.'

'Thanks, Ruth,' Matt said. 'That was thoughtful of you.'

Ruth turned to Kellie. 'You must be exhausted. What a drama to face on your first official day with us.'

'Yes, it was,' Kellie said, looking down at herself ruefully. 'That's the longest run I've ever been on. Next time I'm going to take an overnight backpack just in case.'

Ruth gave her a rueful look. 'I did warn you things can happen out here in the blink of an eye.'

'Yes, well, I'm a believer now,' Kellie said as they made their way to Ruth's car.

The clinic was fully booked so Ruth dropped off Matt before taking Kellie to the Montgomerys' cottage so she could get changed and drive herself back to town.

By the time Kellie made it back to the clinic the waiting room was full. Every available chair was taken and three male patients were standing. A small child was howling piteously in one corner, his harried mother doing what she could to placate him while nursing an infant at her breast.

Trish gave Kellie a relieved smile as she ended the call she was on. 'Welcome to Mayhem Medical Clinic,' she said. 'I know you're not going to believe this, but it's not always as busy as this.'

Kellie straightened her shoulders. 'I'm ready for a challenge,' she said. 'That's why I'm here.'

'Good,' Trish said, handing her the file on top of the stack on the reception counter. 'Angela Baker is your first patient. You won't get much more challenging than that.'

Kellie suppressed a frown, hoping the patient hadn't overheard Trish's comments. She hadn't appeared to, although perhaps it was because her son was now having a full-on tantrum in the middle of the waiting-room floor.

'Angela?'

The young flustered woman got to her feet, almost dropping the baby in the process.

'Here,' Kellie said as she reached for the baby and the nappy bag the young mother was carrying. 'Let me help you.'

'Thanks,' Angela mumbled as she reached for one of her toddler's flailing arms. 'Come on, Charlie. It's time to see the doctor.'

The little boy opened his mouth even wider, his reddened eyes streaming with tears. Kellie felt sorry for both the toddler and his poor mother, who looked like she was close to tears herself. She looked far too thin for someone who had not long had a baby. Her cheeks were sunken and her hair looked like it hadn't seen a brush in a couple of days at least.

It took a bit of cajoling but eventually Charlie shuffled in with his mother and sat down on the floor to play with the small basket of toys in Tim Montgomery's room.

Kellie was glad she had come to the post with experience as she hadn't had time to check the facilities out first. The room was fairly well equipped and organised in such a way that she didn't think she would have too much trouble finding what she needed.

The baby became restless as it was still hungry so Kellie handed her back to Angela so she could run her eyes over the file to familiarise herself with the young woman's history. There wasn't a great deal of information, apart from the two pregnancies which had both progressed more or less normally. Tim's writing was a little difficult to read in places but she could see that Angela was a nineteen-year-old girl. She wasn't married but lived with the father of her children on the edge of town.

'Right.' Kellie smiled as she looked up from the notes. 'What can I do for you, Angela?'

'I think there's something wrong with Charlie,' Angela said, not quite meeting Kellie's gaze. 'He's been crying a lot and keeps trying to hit the baby.'

'Lucy is, what…?' Kellie glanced at the notes again. 'Just ten weeks old and Charlie is nineteen months old. It's perfectly normal for him to be a little put out by the presence of a new baby. He's had you to himself for all that time. He's only a baby himself so it will take him a little while to adjust, but I'll run a few standard tests to reassure you.'

Charlie was surprisingly obliging when Kellie approached him. She crouched down to his level, brushed back his dark brown hair from his face and told him she was going to see how much he had grown over the past few months.

Once she had finished her examination she handed him one of the more colourful toys and he played contentedly while she turned her attention to Angela and the baby.

Lucy was as cute as a button. Kellie felt every maternal urge pulling cathedral-like bells on her biological clock as she examined the tiny wriggling infant.

Lucy, like her brother, had big brown eyes and beautiful skin. Her weight and length were normal and she even gave Kellie a gummy smile, which sent the clanging bells inside Kellie's head into overdrive.

Once the baby was settled back in Angela's arms Kellie asked a few questions about the young woman's health and diet, suggesting she might need to eat a bit more because she was breastfeeding. 'I imagine it's a difficult time, juggling the needs of two small children, but you need to take care of yourself. I'd like to run a few tests just to make sure your haemoglobin is fine and your thyroid function is normal.' She waited a beat before adding, 'I notice you have a slight tremor in your hands. How long have you had that?'

Angela's eyes moved away from hers. 'I don't know... A little while, I guess...' She brought her head back up after a moment and said somewhat defensively, 'I don't drink. As soon as I knew I was pregnant I stopped.'

'That's good, Angela,' Kellie said with an encouraging smile. 'That was a very sensible thing to do. Alcohol crosses the placenta and it also passes through breast milk so it's best to avoid it.'

'It's hard...you know?' Angela said, looking down at the baby. 'There's no one to help me. Shane doesn't see it as his thing. He thinks it's women's work to look after the kids. I never get a break.'

'Would you be interested in being part of a mothers' group if I set one up?' she asked.

Angela gave a one-shoulder shrug. 'I guess.'

Kellie smiled. 'I'll make some enquiries and let you know.

You'll need to come back and see me if the blood tests show up anything abnormal.'

Once she had drawn up the blood for testing she helped Angela back out to Reception with the children before reaching for the next patient file.

The rest of the morning whizzed by as patient after patient came in and out. Kellie saw Matt only twice, once when she was out at Reception, quizzing Trish on facilities available for an elderly patient, and then again when she went in search of the toilet. He had been coming out of his consulting room and briefly asked how she was settling in.

'Fine,' she said. 'I have a couple of patients I wouldn't mind talking over with you when you've got a minute.'

'Trish usually leaves a thirty-minute gap for lunch so we can go over them then,' he said. 'The kitchen's out the back. I'm not sure if Trish has had time to show you around. It's been a full-on morning due to yesterday's cancellations.'

The thirty-minute gap became a ten-minute one because Kellie was held up with another young single mother who was finding it difficult to cope with her three young children. Kellie spent most of the consultation handing over tissues as Gracie Young told her of her woes, but it made her all the more determined to try and sort out something for these unfortunate girls.

'I'm sorry I'm late,' Kellie said as she came into the clinic kitchen after seeing Gracie out.

Matt looked up from the paper he was reading. 'That's fine. Trish told me you've seen some of our more difficult patients.'

Kellie frowned as she flicked on the still warm kettle. 'Where is Trish now?' she asked.

'I think she said something about going to the general store for something,' he answered. 'Why?'

She leaned her hips back against the counter and faced him. 'She made a comment about a patient that I thought was a little inappropriate,' she said. 'The waiting room was full and anyone could have heard. The patient hinted that she had heard it as apparently it's quite a common occurrence.'

'Which patient was it?'

'Angela Baker.'

'Do you want me to have a word with Trish about it?' he asked.

She let out a sigh as the kettle clicked off. 'I probably need to talk to her myself.'

'Angela is a hard case, Kellie,' he said. 'Gracie Young is even worse. They both have pretty sad backgrounds, lots of violence and drinking while they were growing up.

'She told me she's stopped drinking.'

His expression took on a cynical edge. 'And you believed her?'

Kellie stood up straighter. 'Yes, I did, as a matter of fact,' she said. 'She loves those kids. She's doing the best she can. It's not easy for her, you know.'

'You won't be able to fix anything in the short time you're here,' he said, lifting his cup to drain its contents.

'As far as I can see, no one is doing anything to turn things around.' She threw back.

Matt stood up and pushed in his chair. 'Listen, Kellie,' he said. 'You're not a social worker or a psychologist or indeed a drug and alcohol counsellor. You're a GP. Your job is to diagnose and treat illness. You'll end up doing more harm than good.'

'I want to start a support group for the young mothers,' she said with a defiant jut of her chin. 'Once or twice a week for just a couple of hours for them to have a cup of tea or coffee together and chat, sort of like a playgroup. I can do some workshops on parenting or cooking classes even. Anything will be better than nothing.'

'I don't want to rain on your campaign to save the world but you really would be wasting your time,' he said. 'Before you're in the air on your way home they will go back to what they're familiar with.'

'How can you be so cynical?' she asked. 'You've lived out here for this long—surely you realise the issues they face?'

'Of course I do, and I do what I can when I can,' he said as he went to the sink to rinse his cup. 'It's heartbreaking to see the destruction of so many young lives.'

'Is there a community centre I could use?'

Matt turned to look at her. 'You really are serious about this, aren't you?'

Her brown eyes glinted with determination. 'Yes.'

He shoved his hands in his pockets, to stop himself from reaching to brush back a wayward strand of her hair off her face. She looked strong and determined but that chestnut strand lying across her left eyebrow gave her a look of endearing vulnerability. Even the pillowed softness of her mouth made him want to bend his head to press his lips against hers. 'All right, I'll see what I can do,' he said, but somehow his voice came out a little croaky.

She smiled and before he could do anything to stop it— even if he had wanted to—she reached up on tiptoe and pressed a little soft-as-a-summer-breeze kiss to his cheek. 'Thank you, Matt.'

His eyes locked on hers, the silence stretching and stretching until Matt thought the room would burst. He knew he should say something but he couldn't get his mind into gear.

He was standing too close to her. Her perfume had bewitched him. He could feel the drugging of his senses as each pulsing second passed.

'I hope I'm not interrupting anything,' Trish said in a sing-song tone as she came in carrying a packet of tea bags.

'No, not at all,' Matt said brusquely, stepping away from Kellie. 'We were just discussing Angie Baker.'

Trish's gaze flicked to Kellie's before returning to Matt's. 'Oh?'

'I know you've had some run-ins with Angie in the past, but I would prefer it if you'd refrain from making your opinions of her public,' he said. 'That's not how this practice is run.'

Trish's mouth tightened for a moment before she released it on a sigh. 'I'm sorry,' she said. 'You're right, of course. I just get *so* frustrated. David and I spent years trying to have a child and it never happened. She just seems to fall pregnant just looking at a man.'

Matt gave her shoulder a little pat. 'Don't be too hard on yourself, Trish. You're doing a great job. Thanks for resched-uling all those patients yesterday. I owe you.'

'Then promise you'll come to this year's bachelors' and spinsters' ball,' Trish said. 'You never been to one before and it's about time you did.'

'I'll think about it,' he said.

'Will you come too, Kellie?' Trish asked with a broad smile. 'You'd have a great time, I'm sure. People come in from miles around.'

'It sounds like fun,' Kellie said. 'When is it?'

'It's next month,' Trish said, 'I'll give you an invitation with all the details on. You'll have a great time and, you never know, you might even meet the love of your life. Believe me, it's happened before. We've had four marriages in four years so you never know whose turn it will be next.'

Kellie carefully avoided looking at Matt in case he saw the blush she could feel creeping along her cheeks. 'I can't see that happening,' she said. 'Besides, I'm not intending to stay out here any longer than six months.'

Trish's hazel eyes began to twinkle as she bustled out to answer the phone. 'You'll have to change her mind, Matt,' she said over her shoulder. 'I'm sure if you put your mind to it, you could do it.'

There was a flicker of irritation in Matt's gaze as it met Kellie's. 'Don't take any notice of her,' he said. 'She, along with just about everybody else in town thinks it's time I found myself a wife. I'm sorry if you were embarrassed by her— she means well in spite of her rather obvious and clumsy attempt to matchmake.'

'It's all right,' Kellie said. 'I understand. I have heaps of friends and colleagues who do the same thing to me. I've been on so many blind dates over the past few years I reckon I could almost qualify for a guide dog.'

The smile that pulled at his mouth made Kellie's heart skip in her chest. It made his dark blue eyes soften and the tight set to his jaw disappear completely.

He held her gaze for a moment or two before turning away, his smile gradually fading. 'I have patients to see,' he said in a gruff tone.

Kellie drew in a breath and let it out in a long unsteady exhalation as the door clicked shut on his exit. *You're in deep trouble, my girl*, she thought as she tipped her undrunk tea down the sink.

CHAPTER ELEVEN

AFTER she had finished at the clinic Kellie called in at the general store to pay for the things Ruth had bought on her behalf.

Cheryl Yates introduced herself and showed her around the store. 'Of course, it's not up to your city standards, but if you want anything special I can order it in,' she said. 'We're not flash but we're friendly.'

'Thanks, Cheryl.'

Cheryl narrowed her gaze as she looked in the mirror positioned above the cash register. 'Would you excuse me for a moment, Dr Thorne?'

'Sure,' Kellie said, and watched as Cheryl sternly approached a youth of about fifteen who was lingering near the back of the store.

'OK, Ty Smithton,' Cheryl's broad twang bounced off the walls. 'What have you got in your pockets this time?'

'Nuffin', Mrs Yates. I got nuffin.'

'You want me to call the cops or do you want to deal directly with me?' she asked, placing her hands on her hips in a don't-mess-with-me manner.

Kellie couldn't help feeling a carload of burly cops might be preferable to facing the ire of the large-framed woman. The youth scowled and emptied his pockets just as someone came into the store.

'What's going on, Cheryl?' Matt asked.

'Ty here decided he wanted to borrow a few items but he's since changed his mind,' Cheryl said as she escorted the boy to the front door. 'Haven't you, Ty?'

Ty's expression was all brooding surly teenager but Kellie could see beyond it to the lost little boy inside. He reminded her of her brother Nick who had often wound up in trouble in an effort to draw attention to himself.

'How's it going with Mrs Williams looking after you guys?' Matt asked Ty.

'All right, I s'pose,' the boy mumbled.

He gave Ty's shoulder a quick squeeze. 'Go easy on her, mate,' he said. 'She's not as young as your mum, you know.'

'I know…'

Kellie stepped forward. 'Hi, Ty, I'm Kellie Thorne, the new doctor in town. I was thinking about coming to visit Ruth at your place. I can give you a lift if you like then you can show me the way.'

'All right,' Ty said in a grudging tone. 'But it's not far. I can easily walk.'

'Then why don't we do that?' she suggested. 'I need the exercise. I've been cooped up inside all day. A walk in the fresh air is just what I need, and I have no idea where your house is. Ruth did tell me but I've completely forgotten.'

The boy gave an indifferent shrug, which Kellie took to be an affirmative. She turned to Cheryl and snatched up three chocolate bars from the counter. 'I'll take these as well,' she said with a little smile as she handed over some money.

Cheryl turned to Matt once Kellie had left the store with the boy at her side. 'Pretty little thing, isn't she?' she commented.

'Stop it, Cheryl,' he growled. 'You're starting to sound like Trish. I'm sure Tim and Claire have colluded with her about appointing Dr Thorne. In fact, I think the whole town's been in on it. Everywhere I go people give me a knowing look.'

'But she *is* very pretty,' she said. 'And it's well and truly time you moved on. You're young, Matt. Too young to be denying yourself a bit of fun. Why don't you ask her out to your place for a meal?'

Matt schooled his features into a blank mask. 'I'm not interested.'

Cheryl chuckled as she handed him the groceries she had got ready for him earlier. 'You can't fool me, Matt, any more than Ty Smithton or his wayward brothers can. You're interested all right, it's just your head hasn't caught up with your body and your heart.'

Matt frowned as he made his way back to his car. He didn't want to be interested but he just couldn't help it. Kellie was like a magnet he couldn't resist. He felt himself being drawn towards her in spite of his efforts to keep his distance. She exuded life and hope and joy. He had never met someone with such an exuberant boots-and-all mentality before. She went at everything like a bull at a gate, which made him realise how much he had shut himself away over the years. He was lonely, there was no point denying it. He craved the easy companionship of a secure relationship, having been denied it during his formative years.

Madeleine had been so stable, so dependable and reliable.

But totally predictable, a little voice piped up, seemingly from nowhere.

He got behind the wheel and gripped it with both hands until his knuckles turned white.

He *liked* predictable, at least in his private life. He liked knowing what was going to happen next.

Matt couldn't imagine Kellie being predictable, or at least not from what he had seen from her so far. She was impulsive, for one thing. Her scheme to bring the single mothers together was well meaning but fraught with disaster. She was new to the community. She had no idea of how things worked out here. She would no doubt go in with all her social-conscience guns blazing and end up with some of her bullets ricocheting back to hurt her.

He gunned the engine and put the car into gear. It wasn't his problem if she got hurt. What did he care? He had only met her a couple of days ago. She was a city chick who was here for six months and six months only.

But somehow as he drove towards his property he couldn't quite rid himself of the image of Kellie walking alongside the spotty-faced, scowling Ty Smithton. She had taken the time to stop and speak in a respectful way to a troubled young boy who was hell bent on ruining his life. She hadn't turned up her nose or shrunk away in fear. She had faced the young boy as an equal and asked him to help her.

The least Matt could do was support her during the time she was here, which reminded him he had promised to organise for someone to fix that sticking window.

No reason why it couldn't be him.

Kellie couldn't believe the chaos at the Smithtons' house. Ruth had clearly made some headway but there was still a lot to be done. There was a roomful of clothes that had been washed and dried but not sorted. Kellie had never seen such a mould-ridden bathroom and the boys' rooms were like war zones.

Ruth was clearly finding it harder than she had expected and communicated that once the boys had retreated to their rooms. 'I can't believe how messy they are,' she said as she wiped the benchtops yet again. 'I no sooner clean up after them and they're at it again. *And eat!* I can't believe what they can put away.'

'They're boys and they're fully loaded with testosterone,' Kellie said, 'It's entirely normal for them to eat like gannets, believe me.'

Ruth gave a sigh. 'Tegan was the opposite. She hardly ate a thing, especially after I married Dirk. I often wonder if things would have been different…you know, if I hadn't gone ahead with the marriage. Tegan missed her father—he died when she was eight. I was lonely and then Dirk came along and we got along quite well. I hadn't worked since before Tegan was born so I think I might have been looking for security more than anything. It was a disaster from the word go.'

'Stepparenting is a difficult task for most people,' Kellie offered.

'Yes,' Ruth said, sighing again. 'Dirk wasn't the most patient of men and he had rather strict ideas on what girls should and shouldn't do. There have been rumours over the years that he had something to do with her disappearance but I wouldn't have thought him capable of something like that. But even now I lie awake at night and wonder if I missed something somewhere.'

'I really don't know how you've remained so strong,' Kellie said.

'The first few years were the worst,' Ruth said. 'Dirk passed away eighteen months after Tegan disappeared. He had a massive heart attack. I had to keep myself together in case Tegan came back. I kept thinking what if she had run away and then came back only to find her mother had given up on life? I could so easily have ended it all. I wanted to end the torture of not knowing but I think I'm finally coming to terms with the fact that I might never know the truth.'

'I think it's amazing how you help people in spite of your own suffering,' Kellie said. 'Look at what you've done for Julie and the boys for instance.'

'I spoke to Julie this afternoon and her hand is recovering well,' Ruth said. 'She is being released the day after tomorrow.'

After she had helped Ruth bring some sort of order to the house and spent a few minutes helping the youngest boy, Cade, with his homework, Kellie asked if the three boys were interested in doing some yard work for her.

Ty, the oldest at fifteen, grunted something unintelligible but fourteen-year-old Rowan and twelve-year-old Cade showed a bit of interest, although it was somewhat guarded.

'I thought it might be nice for when Dr and Mrs Montgomery come back if the garden was spruced up a bit.' Kellie explained her plan. 'I know the drought makes things difficult, but if we start now there are still things that can be done to make the place look neat and tidy by the time they return.'

'Are you going to pay us, Dr Thorne?' Cade asked with a wary expression.

'Of course!' Kellie said. 'There's no such thing as a free lunch, right?'

She told them how much she was prepared to pay them and arranged to meet them at the Montgomerys' house on Saturday morning.

Driving into the Montgomerys' driveway a few minutes later, she caught sight of a slinking shape near the rainwater tank at the side of the house. At first she thought it might have been a fox or even a dingo, but when it moved away into the shadows of the night she could see its tail was long and thin not bushy and the colour not golden but more like a patch-work of brown and black and white.

She turned on the back light once she got inside and looked out over the yard but there was no sign of any movement.

A few minutes later her mobile phone rang just as she had taken her last mouthful of her daily allowance of chocolate. 'Hello?' she answered from a full mouth.

'Kellie, it's Matt…' He paused for moment. 'Have I caught you having dinner?'

'No, I had a snatch-and-grab meal with Ruth and the boys. That was my chocolate hit for the day. What can I do for you?'

There was a little silence.

She heard him draw in a deep breath before he spoke. 'I promised to fix that window for you. When would be a convenient time?'

'I thought you were going to get someone else to fix it. I didn't realise you were going to do it yourself.'

'I had to do the same to one of the windows at my place a while back,' he said. 'It's no trouble really.'

'What about tomorrow after work?' she suggested. 'That way I can cook you dinner in payment.'

'I don't expect to be paid,' he said quickly.

'Nevertheless, I insist on cooking you a meal. Besides, you'll be doing me a favour by keeping me company for a few hours. I'm not used to being on my own in such a quiet house. It's sort of creeping me out.'

'Perhaps a dog might be a good idea after all,' he said. 'I've heard there's one hanging about the school, looking for scraps.'

'I think it was here when I got home a while ago. I saw it slink around the back of the tank.'

'You could leave out some food for it and see if it's friendly,' he said. 'But don't approach it unless you're sure. It might take a nip at you.'

'I'll be careful,' she promised.

There was another silence.

'Well…' he said. 'I'd better let you get some sleep. It's been a rough couple of days for you. You must be totally wiped out.'

'I'm pretty used to hard work.'

'You'll certainly get plenty of it out here. You'll have to run the clinic singlehandedly tomorrow as I'm flying out to do the clinic at Warradunga Crossing.'

'You don't need me to come with you?' she asked.

'Although the appointment book isn't full, I thought you'd be better to stay in town in case there's anything urgent,' he said. 'The clinic at the Crossing isn't a big one.'

'And I don't suppose the plane is either, right?'

Matt felt a smile tug at his mouth. 'Not as big as the ones you're used to but it does the job.'

'So what time will you get back?'

'About five,' he said. 'I'll go home, have a shower and get back to your place at about seven, unless you want me to come later?'

'No, that will be fine.'

'Good. I'll look forward to it.'

Not as much as I will, Kellie thought as she placed her phone back on the kitchen bench.

Her skin lifted in a faint shiver of anticipation. She knew the old adage about the way to a man's heart being through his stomach might not apply to someone like Matt McNaught, but she was going to have a damn good try.

CHAPTER TWELVE

KELLIE was putting the last-minute touches to her make-up when she heard the sound of Matt knocking on the front door. She put the pot of lipgloss down and quickly slipped on her high heels and click-clacked her way down the hall.

She opened the door wide and smiled. 'Hi.'

Matt felt as if he had been zapped with a stun gun. He stood there for several seconds, trying to keep his jaw from dropping at the vision of loveliness in front of him. She was wearing a red-and-white sundress with shoestring straps, nipped in at the waist with a shiny patent-leather belt, emphasising her trim body. Her hair was loose about her shoulders; she had done something to enhance the slight wave in it, the cascade of bouncy curls framing her heart-shaped face giving her a casual but elegant look. She smelt of summer, the delicate notes of honeysuckle—or was it orange blossom?—danced around his nostrils like invisible sprites.

'Um…won't you come in?' she asked.

'Er…right,' he said, stepping over the threshold and thrusting a bottle of wine at her. 'I don't know if you like red or white but this is from the Roma vineyard. I thought you might like to try it. It's the oldest vineyard in Queensland. It began in 1863.'

'I've heard of it,' she said, and closed the door. 'I'll open the wine while you play handyman with the window. I got the bedroom one open the other night but it's still a little stiff.'

Yeah, well, it's not the only thing feeling that way, Matt thought as she brushed past him. He was glad he was holding his toolkit so he could hide his physical reaction to her.

He went through the house and checked each window, listening to her singing along to the CD player. She had a nice voice, light and pure and enthusiastic as she was about seemingly everything.

I wonder what she's like in bed.

The thought was like an intruder inside his head. He tried to evict it but it wouldn't leave. It made it even worse when the last window he had to check was in her bedroom. The intoxicating fragrance of her permeated everything. Even the lightweight curtains smelt of her as he pulled them aside to work the latch.

'How's it going?' she asked from just behind him.

Matt hadn't heard her approach and nicked his finger on the blade of the chisel. 'Er…fine,' he said. 'I'm just about done.'

Kellie frowned when he turned around and began to wind his finger around his handkerchief. 'Have you cut yourself?' she asked.

'It's just a scratch.'

'Let me see.'

'It's nothing,' he said. 'I told you, it's just a little scratch. It will stop bleeding in a second.'

Kellie gave him a reproving look as she reached for his hand. 'You don't need to go all macho on me, Matt,' she said. 'If I can handle what Julie Smithton did to her finger, I think I'll cope with what you've done with yours.'

She unpeeled the handkerchief and inspected the flesh wound. 'Mmm,' she said. 'It looks like it needs some pressure for a bit longer. I'll cleanse it for you and put on a sticky plaster.'

'There's really no need…'

Her eyes met his. 'Why are you being so stubborn about such a little thing?' she asked. 'When was the last time you allowed someone to help *you* for a change?'

He held her gaze for a moment or two. 'All right,' he said, blowing out of sigh of resignation. 'Do what you need to do. I won't put up a struggle.'

Kellie led him by the hand to the bathroom and making him sit on a small stool, attended to his finger with meticulous care. She was acutely aware of his long legs, she had to step around them a couple of times to reach the first-aid cupboard. She was also intensely aware of his hand in hers as she cleansed and dressed the wound. She imagined how it would feel to have those strong, long-fingered hands on her body, touching her face, tilting her head to claim her mouth with his own…

Matt met her brown gaze on a level. She was wearing mascara, which made her long eyelashes even more lustrous. His eyes went to her mouth. This close he could see the tiny sparkles in her lipgloss, making her lips all the more tempting to taste. He watched as the point of her tongue sneaked out to paste a film of moisture on top of the gloss and his insides gave a sudden kick of reaction. It would be so easy to lean forward and—

'There,' she said briskly, scrunching up the wrapping of the sticky plaster. 'I'm all done.'

Matt got to his feet. 'Thank you, but it was totally unnecessary to go to all that fuss over nothing.'

'It wasn't nothing and, besides, I didn't want you to bleed all over the place. Imagine if Tim and Claire come back to find bloodstains all over their bedroom carpet?'

'Good point.'

She turned from the basin, where she had been washing her hands. 'Ready for dinner now?'

'Sure.'

Kellie led the way to the kitchen where she had an Italian chicken dish simmering. She poured two glasses of wine and handed him one. 'Thanks for fixing the windows. I really appreciate it. I'm hopeless at household maintenance. I guess it comes from living with six men. They did that sort of stuff while Mum and I got on with the cooking and housework.'

He took the glass with a brief brush of his fingers against hers. 'Did you resent having to do that?'

She cradled her glass in her hands. 'Not at first. I took over the cooking when Mum got sick. It was hard once she'd gone to stop doing it. Dad and the boys were devastated. The last thing they needed was a huge shopping list and a week's menu thrust in their hands.'

Matt thought about how caring she was, how she had put her needs aside for the sake of her father and younger brothers. 'All the same, it must have been hard, not having a life of your own,' he said. 'What about boyfriends and so on? How did you juggle your professional and social life with your family taking up so much of your time?'

Her smooth brow furrowed slightly. 'It wasn't easy. I'm nearly thirty years old and I've only had one lover. I guess you think that's pretty pathetic, huh?'

He felt his mouth tip upwards in a rueful smile. 'I'm hardly one to criticise. I haven't exactly been out there sowing my wild oats.'

She smiled back at him but he noticed her cheeks were a little pink. 'I guess I should check on dinner...'

Matt watched as she deftly sorted out plates and garnishes and steamed vegetables as if it was second nature to her. He couldn't help wondering what she would think of his micro-waved single-serve meals or his two-recipe repertoire of macaroni cheese or savory mince on toast. 'You obviously enjoy cooking,' he said into the silence.

'I love it,' she said handing him a plate loaded with food.

'Was your mother a good cook?' he asked once they were both seated at the small pine table.

'She was fabulous,' she said, passing him the pepper grinder. 'I stood on a step-stool by her side for as long as I can remember. I think she would have loved to have been a chef but she didn't get the opportunity. She got pregnant with me while she was at college so that put an end to that.'

'Was she bitter about it?'

She met his gaze across the table. 'No, of course not. She loved being a mother.'

He looked into the contents of his glass. 'My mother was the opposite. She also fell pregnant by mistake but it was made very clear to my father and me that it had ruined her life.'

Kellie felt her heart contract. 'Did she tell you that?'

He forked up some of the casserole. 'I seem to remember it was a recurrent theme before she finally left.'

'You must have been so hurt.'

He gave an indifferent shrug. 'I don't dwell on it much. It happened and I can't change it. My father, on the other hand, lets it eat away at him even now. He hasn't moved on. He talks about nothing else whenever I call him, which isn't often. He can't seem to accept that she's not coming back.'

'And you don't think you're a little bit like him in that regard?'

He frowned as he met the challenge of her gaze. 'What are you saying?'

She put down her fork and picked up her wineglass. 'If you can't see it, I'm not going to hit you over the head with it.'

His frown deepened. 'I suppose by that you mean Madeleine.'

'You're still carrying a photo of her in your wallet,' Kellie said. 'You have a shrine built to her in your home. You visit her parents every year on her birthday. If that doesn't demonstrate how stuck you are then what will?'

'I can hardly wipe her from my memory as if she never was a part of my life,' he bit out.

'No, of course not, but I'm sure she wouldn't have wanted you to live the way you are doing,' Kellie argued.

'You know nothing of how I live my life.' *Or how I'm about to change it*, he added silently.

She gave him a wry look. 'Going on what I've seen so far, I think I've got a pretty clear idea.'

He put down his knife and fork, his top lip lifting mockingly. 'So you think you can do something about my sad and sorry situation, do you, Dr Thorne?'

Kellie kept her eyes trained on his. 'I don't see anything wrong in you getting out a bit more, having some fun, dating now and again. What harm would it do?'

He leaned back in his chair, still with his mouth tilted. 'So is this what this is all about?' He waved his hand over the meal between them. 'Is this yet another one of your do-good missions to achieve while you're here?'

Kellie frowned at the veiled insult he had thrown at her. 'I know you think I'm wasting my time with Angie and Gracie but it's not just the young mums around here that need help. Julie's boys do, too. They're bored and restless, that's why they're in trouble all the time. They have low self-esteem and the only way they can get attention is to do something bad. I've arranged for them to do something good for a change. They're coming to help me here on Saturday to clean up the yard a bit. Who knows? It might inspire them to do the same at their house or others in the area.'

Matt looked at the bright sparks of enthusiasm in her eyes and wondered when the last time had been that he had been passionate about anything, *truly* passionate. For most of his life he had taken a back seat when it had come to eagerness. Every time he had been excited about something he had been let down. He remembered one time, not long after his mother had left, he'd thought he'd seen her coming up the front path. He had dashed downstairs, his heart beating like a bass drum in his chest, only to throw open the door to see it was a complete stranger, selling raffle tickets for a charity. The disappointment had been totally devastating. He hadn't realised until then how much he had hoped his life would go back to what it had been. But it was never going to go back and it was up to him now to move forward.

'You think I'm wasting my time, don't you?' she asked.

Matt picked up his wineglass and twirled the contents. 'I think you mean well but you're likely to get swamped with the endless needs of people you can't help in any significant way.'

'I don't care about the destination as much as the journey,' she said. 'I know I haven't got long here but just the fact that someone is taking the time and making the effort to make a difference in someone's life is surely a worthwhile enterprise.'

He put his glass down and met her brown eyes. 'Even if you get hurt in the process?'

'I'd rather get hurt trying. At least it proves I care, and it could make a difference, maybe in just one life but it's still worth it.'

A warm feeling spread like heated honey through Matt's chest as he held her gaze. 'Do you make it a habit to nurture absolutely everyone who crosses your path?' he asked.

She gave him a self-conscious smile. 'It's my mother

complex. It's showing, isn't it? I just can't seem to help it. I pick up every lame duck or stray. I've been doing it since I was a little kid.'

'Speaking of strays, I thought I saw that dog you were talking about on my way to the front door,' Matt said. 'It was sniffing around the tank stand. I forgot to tell you earlier.' *Only because I was completely taken aback by your amazingly sexy appearance*, he tacked on mentally.

'I left some food and water out at the bottom of the back veranda,' she said. 'I hope it hangs around now. That way I can gradually teach it to trust me.'

'My dog Spike was from the dogs' home,' he said. 'He had been treated cruelly by some idiot who thought a working dog should be confined to a small back yard in the city. The guy had him tied up day in, day out and whenever Spike made a sound he would get whipped with whatever was handy.'

'Oh that's terrible,' Kellie gasped. 'How can people be so cruel?'

He gave her a grim look. 'I don't know, but animal cruelty is one thing that truly sickens me.'

'Me, too,' she said with fervour. 'And children. I hate the thought of little kids being hurt. There are so many people who are desperate to have kids and yet others treat their children like punching bags. Why have kids if you can't be patient and loving towards them?'

'Do you want kids?' Matt asked, surprising himself at asking such a candid question.

He watched as her eyes moved away from his, her index finger absently running round the rim of her glass. 'I think there are a few women out there who genuinely don't want to have children,' she said. 'But while I have yet to meet someone who has regretted having a child, I have met plenty who have regretted they didn't.' She brought her eyes back to his. 'You were right about the fertility-issue thing we talked about the other day. It seems harder than ever to find a man who wants to settle down and have kids. If you date a man the same age as you they don't want kids until it's too late for you. If you date someone older they often have kids from a previous relationship so you end up trying to convince him to have another child when he hardly has enough to pay for the ones he has.'

'It sounds like you've thought about this at length.'

She gave him another self-conscious smile. 'I'm on the fast train to thirty,' she said. 'I try not to panic that I might not meet someone in time, but it's hard not to think about it.'

'Is that why you came out here—in the hope of meeting someone?'

Kellie chewed at her lip before answering. 'Not really, I just felt I needed a change. My ex-boyfriend was two-timing me, and like most women in that situation I was the very last to find out. I didn't think Newcastle was big enough for me to lick my wounds in private so I took the first job I saw advertised.'

'So it could just as easily have been Outer Mongolia or Culwulla Creek,' he said with a hint of a wry smile.

She smiled back at him. 'Yes, I suppose so. But just as well it was here as it would have cost me a fortune in excess baggage.'

'Were you in love with your boyfriend?' he asked.

Kellie found his blue gaze suddenly intense and had to lower hers a fraction. 'I'm not sure if I know what it feels like to be in love,' she confessed as she gathered up their plates, 'or at least not personally. I know my mother and father loved each other from the moment they met, but I didn't love Harley that way. I liked his company and we had interests in common but…'

'But?' he prompted as he followed her to the sink with their used glasses.

She brought her eyes back to his. 'But I think something important was missing. I think I realised it from the word go but I was so keen to find someone I ignored it. And then when I found about how he was seeing someone else…well, that was just the boost my ego needed. He even told me it was my fault for not being attractive enough to hold his interest.'

'Yes, well, like I said the other day, Kellie, he was a king-sized jerk,' Matt said, looking down at her mouth. He knew it was a mistake to do so but he couldn't resist the temptation. Her lips were so damned kissable, so soft and supple. A few strands of her chestnut hair had moved forward over her left eyebrow and without even realising he was doing it his hand came out and gently tucked them behind the shell-like curve of her ear.

He watched as she gave a tiny shiver. He felt her tremble against his fingers as they trailed down from her ear over the smooth curve of her jaw to her chin, her brown eyes darkening to the colour of melted chocolate as she looked up at him with uncertainty and vulnerability in her gaze.

Matt could feel his heartbeat, like an out-of-control time-piece in his chest, speeding up, slowing down, skipping a beat here and there and then speeding up again. His breathing became shallow and uneven and his skin prickled all over with the need to feel more of her.

With two of his fingers still beneath her chin, he lifted her face as he lowered his until his mouth touched down on hers, the soft pillow of her lips sending a jolt of reaction coursing through him like a zap of lightning. She tasted of wine and feminine want, her tongue meeting the first explorative stroke of his with electrifying heat.

The kiss took on a life of its own. He had no hope of controlling his response to her mouth under the pressure of his. It was like an uncontrollable bush fire. It had started with a flicker but was now racing away, consuming everything in its path. He felt himself being swept away on a tide of such intense longing he thought he was going to make a complete and utter fool of himself. His body was already fit to explode, the quickening of his blood engorging him to bursting point. Surely she could feel it against her? There was no way of disguising his reaction, she only had to reach down between their tightly locked bodies and examine it for herself. The thought of her doing so made him kiss her with increasing ardour.

He wanted her.

He drove his tongue even deeper into the moist cave of her mouth and groaned.

God forgive him for being human but he *wanted* her…

CHAPTER THIRTEEN

KELLIE had never been kissed so thoroughly in her life. She had never felt such fervour in a man's lips and tongue, or such incredible need and purpose. His mouth was like a hot brand on hers, searing hers, making her weak with longing. Her body felt the hard probe of his erection, the hot surge of his body making her feel feminine and dizzyingly alive in a way she had never felt before.

His mouth was still locked on hers as his hands moved to her hips, pulling her even tighter against the intimate connection of their bodies. She felt his fingers dig into the curve of her bottom, intensifying their contact to the point where her feminine core pulsed with ripples of desire to feel him fill her, to claim her as his. She rubbed against him enticingly, wanting him, needing him to satisfy the need he and he alone had awakened.

As if someone had flicked a switch in his head he suddenly put her from him, his expression stripped of all emotion as he moved away from her to pace the kitchen.

'M-Matt?'

He shoved a hand through his hair, making it even more disordered than her hands had done moments previously. 'That should never have happened,' he said in a gruff tone, his eyes avoiding hers. 'I'm sorry. I don't want to give you the wrong impression.'

Kellie swallowed to give herself a moment to gather her scattered senses into some semblance of order. 'Are you saying you didn't want to kiss me?' she asked.

He turned around to look at her. 'I'm not going to waste my time denying I didn't want to kiss you but…' He sent his hand through his hair again. 'But I'm not interested in taking this any further.'

Kellie pressed her lips together, trying to quell the ache of disappointment deep inside her being. 'Madeleine's not coming back, Matt,' she said, before she could stop herself. 'She's not coming back, and denying yourself a full life isn't going to bring her back.'

She heard him suck in a harsh breath as he swung away from her. 'Do you think I don't know she's not coming back?' he barked at her. 'I was the one who identified her at the bloody morgue. Don't tell me what I already know.'

Kellie stepped forward to grasp one of his arms. 'But have you accepted it, Matt?' she asked. 'You want to move on, I know you do, but you just won't let yourself.'

He brushed off her hand as if it were a mosquito. 'Stop analysing me, Kellie. Can't you tell rejection when you hear it? I am not interested. Got that? *Not in-ter-ested.*' He drew out the syllables for emphasis.

Kellie felt tears sting her eyes. 'I don't believe you. You just kissed me as if your life depended on it. Your whole body was shaking with desire. Don't insult me by denying it.'

His eyes blazed at her. 'It was a mistake, damn you! You look at me with those big brown eyes of yours and I swear to God any man married, celibate or dead from the waist up would want to kiss you.'

'But you're not married or dead from the waist up. I know that for a fact.'

He frowned at her. 'Stop this, stop it now. I am not going to be drawn into an affair with you just to stroke your ego after being ditched by your two-timing boyfriend.'

Kellie glared at him in affront. 'Is that what you think this is about?'

He sent her a cynical glance. 'You've been hurt and you went bush. It's totally understandable you'd latch onto the first available man to salve your pride.'

She injected her tone with venom. 'And you think I've selected *you* as the first step in my relationship rehab?'

Matt held her fiery gaze for several seconds. 'I think you're very vulnerable just now,' he said, his tone now calm and controlled. 'You're new in town, you've got baggage that needs to be dealt with and I don't want to hurt you any more than you've been hurt. You're a nice person, Kellie. I can see that from how you've responded to the needs of the patients you've come into contact with so far. You're a really lovely young woman who deserves much more than I can offer right now.'

She screwed her mouth up, not quite a pout but somewhere close. 'I wish you hadn't kissed me,' she said. 'No one's ever kissed me like that before.'

Matt couldn't stop himself from tipping up her chin until her eyes met his. 'You know something, Kellie? No one's ever kissed me quite like that either.'

'Didn't Madeleine kiss you like that?' she asked softly, her smooth brow wrinkled in a little frown.

Matt should have known the question was coming but for some reason he didn't have a ready answer. The truth was Madeleine had always been a few steps behind him when it had come to their physical relationship. He had put it down to her sheltered upbringing. She had not been comfortable with outward affection, and sleeping together had been a huge step for her, one she had baulked at several times. If he was entirely truthful he would have to admit he'd always had some reservations about their sexual compatibility, but he had thought the security of marriage would sort them out. Madeleine had grown up in a conservative home. Sex outside of marriage was frowned upon so it was no wonder she had always been a little restrained with him.

'Did she?' Kellie asked.

'Did she what?' Matt asked, trying not to stare at the cushioned bow of her mouth.

'Did Madeleine kiss you like I kissed you?'

He stood there looking down at her for endless seconds. 'No,' he said at last. 'No, she didn't.'

'Did she sleep with you?'

Matt felt as if he was betraying Madeleine's memory by revealing the intimate details of their relationship but still he answered, 'We took things slowly but yes, we did eventually sleep together.'

Kellie turned away to clear the rest of the table. 'I wish I hadn't slept with Harley,' she said, clattering the side plates as she stacked them haphazardly. 'Looking back now, I can see I was being used. I wasn't the one he wanted, I was the fill-in—his little bit on the side.' She gave a shudder of revulsion as she stomped back to the kitchen. 'I am *such* an idiot when it comes to men. You'd think after living with six of them I'd be an expert by now but, no, I have to make a complete fool of myself all over again.'

'You haven't made a fool of yourself,' Matt said gently.

She turned from the sink where she had dumped the rest of the plates and looked up at him. 'Are you sure?'

He gave her a crooked smile. 'We kissed. So what?' His tone was deliberately offhand. 'Lots of people do it. It doesn't have to mean anything.'

She lifted up her hand and with the point of her index finger lightly traced the shape of his bottom lip. 'You have a very nice mouth, Dr McNaught, especially when you smile,' she said, her voice coming out in a slightly breathless whisper.

Matt could feel his bottom lip buzzing with sensation all over again. His insides were coiling with need just looking at that pretty uptilted, heart-shaped face. Her lips were still swollen from his kiss, plump and pink and slightly parted, leaving just enough room for him to slide his tongue in and…

Kellie jerked backwards. 'Did you hear that?' she asked in a hushed voice, her eyes suddenly wide with apprehension.

He looked at her blankly. 'Hear what?'

'That noise outside.'

'What noise?'

'I think there's someone outside,' she said, still whispering. 'I thought I heard someone step on the veranda.'

Matt strained to listen but the only thing he could hear was the sound of one of the oleander trees brushing up against the house in the slight breeze. 'I'll have a look around but I'm sure it's just the wind,' he said.

Kellie waited as Matt did a circuit of the house, taking the torch from the cupboard beneath the sink with him. He came back a few minutes later and reassured her that everything was as it should be.

'But I think your stray has eaten the food you put out,' he said. 'That might have been what you heard.'

'I hope you're right,' she said, hugging her arms around herself.

'Are you going to be OK here on your own?' Matt asked.

Kellie pasted a brave smile on her face. 'Of course I'll be OK. I'm still getting used to the house and living on my own for the first time ever. I'll be fine in a couple of days.'

He picked up his keys. 'Call me if you're worried during the night. I'll come straight over.'

'Thanks, but I'm sure I'll be fine,' she said still rubbing her upper arms as if to ward off a chill. 'I'm not normally such a coward. It's just this house has an odd feel to it. I can't put my finger on it. I just feel uncomfortable.'

'Living in someone else's house is a bit weird,' he said. 'You're surrounded by the Montgomerys' belongings instead of your own.'

'I guess you're right…'

'Is it what I said about snakes that spooked you?' he asked. 'You haven't seen one, have you?'

'No, but that's one of the reasons I want to tidy up the yard a bit,' she said. 'That long straggly grass down the back has to go for a start.'

'It's just a normal house, Kellie,' he said. 'A bit neglected, I know but the Montgomerys aren't the house-renovating types. Tim's no handyman and Claire has a chronic problem with her back, which limits what she can do. That's why the garden is the way it is, irrespective of the drought.'

'Who lived here before Tim and Claire?'

'I'm not sure. You'd have to ask someone like Ruth who has lived in the town for most of her life. I do know it was vacant for a long time before the Montgomerys took the post. They bought it for a song, but to tell you the truth I think they'll probably move on once they get back from overseas. Tim hasn't said anything to me but I know Claire is probably going to end up wheelchair-bound so living out here long term is going to be out of the question.'

'So you don't think they'll mind if I clean it up a bit?' she asked. 'It will help them get a better price for it if they want to sell it.'

He smiled one of his fleeting smiles. 'I think it's a nice gesture and they'll appreciate it very much.'

She gave him a bright smile in return. 'And it will kill two...no, *three* birds with one stone. The Smithton boys will gain valuable experience, don't you think?'

'That's if they turn up,' he said with a cynical look.

Her face fell. 'You think they won't show?'

'Ty won't, that's for sure,' he said. 'He's a crime statistic waiting to happen, and Rowan's not much better. As for Cade...well, what sort of role models has he had? He's a nice enough kid but with his brothers in and out of trouble all the time, what hope has he got?'

'I'm not in the habit of giving up on people,' she said. 'I think they will turn up. In fact, I think even Ty will.'

His expression demonstrated he didn't share her view but he softened it saying, 'Thank you for dinner. It's been quite a while since I had a gourmet meal. It was delicious.'

She smiled up at him. 'Thanks for fixing the windows.'

'It was a pleasure.'

Kellie stood there, looking up at him for a beat or two. 'I guess I'll see you at the clinic tomorrow,' she finally said.

His eyes dropped to her mouth for a moment. 'Yes...I expect you will.'

''Night, then...'

His eyes held hers for a little longer than necessary. 'Goodnight, Kellie.'

Kellie watched as he strode down the steps to his car. He didn't look back at her but got into his car and backed out as if he couldn't wait to get away. She watched the red eyes of his taillights disappear into the distance before she let out her breath in one long jagged stream.

'You're only here six months.' She gave herself a little pep talk as she closed and locked the door. 'You don't need the complication of falling in love, understand? So it was a fabulous kiss. So what? There are probably thousands…no, *millions*…of guys who could kiss like that or even better. Matt McNaught is off limits. He's not interested. He told you in no uncertain terms. Do *not* go there.'

For the next few days Kellie concentrated on sorting out the arrangements for using the community centre in between seeing patients. She barely caught a glimpse of Matt—he seemed equally snowed under with a seemingly endless list of patients, including a run of home visits which, due to the distances involved, ate up a lot of time. But even so she couldn't help feeling he was deliberately avoiding having one-on-one time with her, although she knew he had been personally responsible for most of the out-of-hours handyman work done at the community centre. She had seen the paint tins in the back of his car on her way into the clinic and was keen to see him in person to thank him for his support.

'How are your plans going for the mothers' group?' Trish asked as the week drew to a close.

'Their first meeting is next week,' Kellie announced proudly. 'I've organised the delivery of some toys for the little ones to play with while the mothers chat and get to know one another.'

'Gosh, you have been busy,' Trish said. 'Julie Smithton told me you've got her boys coming to help you tomorrow at the Montgomerys' house. She thinks you must have some sort of magic touch when it comes to the male of the species. She can't get them to lift a finger at home.'

Kellie smiled as she picked up the next patient's file. 'I have less than six months to work a miracle. No point wasting time, right?'

'Oh, I almost forgot,' Trish said, reaching over for some blood results and handing them to Kellie. 'These came in this morning. It's Angie Baker's thyroid results.'

Kellie looked at the printout, the raised T4, low TSH and high antithyroid peroxidase antibody levels clearly indicating Graves's disease.

'I'll call her and let her know,' Kellie said. 'She'll have to make a decision about treatment. She won't be able to take medication or radioactive iodine while she's breastfeeding. But surgery when she's got two little ones to look after and not much support would be daunting for her.'

Angie came in later that afternoon looking even more exhausted than previously. Charlie was acting up as usual but as soon as Kellie handed him a bright toy that squeaked when it was squeezed he played quite happily albeit rather noisily, as she discussed Angie's treatment options with her.

'But won't it just go back to normal all by itself?' Angie asked, her dark brown eyes worried.

'That occasionally happens, but usually it just stays over-active, and causes a lot of problems as a result,' Kellie explained. 'It's quite dangerous in the long term to leave hyperthyroidism untreated. It will cause weight loss, heart problems, eye problems, weakness, and make you feel hot, anxious and irritable. We can use blocking medication—sometimes the over-activity goes away after a year or so of treatment, but we'll have to watch your levels with blood tests, and make sure you don't get any eye problems while you're on the tablets, and you'll have to stop breastfeeding.

The other alternatives are radioactive iodine, not a great idea at your age, or surgery to remove the thyroid.'

'I don't want no one slicing my neck open,' Angie said after Kellie had given a brief description of a thyroidectomy.

'I know it sounds very unpleasant,' Kellie said, 'but the scar is barely noticeable after a few months. Most surgeons try and follow the natural crease in the neck.'

'I'll think about it,' Angie said as the baby began to become restless.

Kellie helped her out of the consulting room with Charlie, who had decided he wanted to keep the toy. He clutched it tightly to his little chest and pouted as his mother told him to hand it back.

'Let him keep it,' Kellie said. 'I've ordered some more from Brisbane in any case for the mothers' group and the surgery.'

'It's very kind of you,' Angie said, tucking the baby closer. 'I mean giving that to Charlie as well as what you're doing at the community centre. We've never had anything like that here before.'

'So you think you'll come along with the kids?'

Angie gave her a shy smile. 'Got nothing better to do, have I?'

Kellie smiled back. 'I think it will be a lot of fun. As time goes on we can set up a sort of roster to take turns minding the children while the others have a coffee. It will mean you can each have a little break.'

'Yeah, well, I could really do with one of those,' Angie said wryly, reaching for Charlie, who had slipped out of her grasp and was rapidly heading for the door.

Matt was just coming in and captured the runaway toddler by lifting him up in his arms. 'Hi, there, Charlie,' he said, smiling at the little boy. 'What have you got there?'

Charlie squeezed the toy so it squeaked, his big brown eyes luminous with possessive pride.

'Dr Thorne gave it to him,' Angie said, shyly lowering her gaze.

Matt gave the little boy's back a stroke. 'Hey, you've really grown since I saw you last, little man. How is your baby sister doing?'

Charlie buried his head in Matt's shoulder, the toy still grasped tightly in his hand.

'He loves her to death,' Angie said with a show of dry humour that made Matt smile.

'It's normal, Angie,' he reassured her. 'He's just feeling a little put out that someone else needs you as much if not more than him. How is Shane?'

Angie's gaze dropped even lower. 'I dunno. I haven't seen him since the baby was born. He's gone bush. He started drinking again.'

Kellie felt as if she had been slapped. She'd had no idea Angie's circumstances were so dreadful. She couldn't imagine what it must be like having two tiny infants to look after with absolutely no support from their father. She also felt totally incompetent that she hadn't discovered this information for herself. Why hadn't Angie told her? It made her feel as if she had been remiss in some way, too intent on sorting out Angie's social network without considering the all-important domestic scene.

'Are you still living out at the flats?' Matt was asking.

Angie nodded dejectedly as she patted the fretting baby's back. 'It's not what I want for the kids but what else can I do?' she asked. 'Shane promised he'd look after us but he wants his freedom and to tell you the truth I can hardly blame him. I wouldn't mind a bit of freedom myself.'

Matt glanced at Kellie, who was looking rather pale. He turned back to Angie. 'I'll speak to Ruth Williams about coming round to give you a hand,' he said. 'Julie is back now from her trip to Brisbane so she won't need Ruth's help any more.'

Angie cuddled her children closer. 'I can manage on my own. I don't want no one telling me how to bring up my kids. Anyway, what would she know? Her only kid ran away at fourteen. Some great mother she must have been.'

'Angie,' Matt said in a deep calm voice, 'take the children home and I'll send Ruth round to help you. You can't go on like this, juggling two little ones with little or no support. Ruth loves to help, it's her life. It gives her a purpose. She's on a high after looking after the Smithton boys for a few days. She'll be thrilled to be of use to you, it's just the thing she needs to take her mind off things.'

'We all reckon her Tegan is dead, Dr McNaught,' Angie said. 'The sooner she realises it the better.'

'That is an issue for the police,' Matt said, bending down to pick up Charlie's toy, which he had just dropped, and handing it back to him. 'Anything else is speculation.'

As Angie left the clinic, Kellie whooshed out a sigh heavy enough to lift the strands of her hair that had worked loose from her ponytail.

'Tough day?' Matt asked, watching as she tucked her hair behind her ear.

'You could say that,' she said with another weary sigh. 'I had no idea Angie's partner wasn't on the scene. She never said a word.'

'Don't take it personally, Kellie. A lot of the locals need time to build up trust, especially with authority figures like doctors. She would have told you eventually. For all her problems she still has a sense of pride.'

'She's got Graves's disease,' Kellie said, handing him the blood results from Angie's file.

He read through the pathology for a moment before handing it back. 'Good work,' he said. 'That could easily have been overlooked, especially given her drinking history.'

'Matt, thanks for what you've been doing at the community centre,' she said. 'The paint job looks great.'

He gave an offhand shrug. 'I had nothing better to do.'

There was a short silence.

'Well…' Kellie said with forced brightness. 'I'd better get going. It's been a long week.'

Matt thought of the weekend stretching ahead of him, the long lonely hours of catching up with paperwork and farm accounts with only the dust and flies to keep him company.

Ever since they'd had dinner together the other night he had felt increasingly lonely. Kissing Kellie had been a stupid mistake for it had awakened feelings and urges in him that were now torturing him day and night. Even looking at her now, with her hair all awry, her eyes shadowed with tiredness, he wanted to haul her into his arms and feel that soft mouth move with passion beneath his. He wanted to feel the duck and dart of her tongue playing with his, teasing him, tantalising him. He had been a fool to tell her he wasn't interested. Of course he was interested. It was just that he wanted to take things slowly, to get to know her, to spend time with her away from the prying eyes of the small bush community.

He brushed an imaginary fly away from his face and stepped past her before he gave into the temptation to pull her in to his arms. 'See you on Monday,' he said curtly.

CHAPTER FOURTEEN

KELLIE looked at the empty bowl on the back step of the veranda the next morning and smiled. Her smile grew even wider when she answered the knock at the front door to find all three Smithton boys standing there.

Ty was leaning indolently against the veranda rail, his demeanour that of a typical bored teenager who looked as if he had only come under duress.

'Hi, guys,' Kellie said cheerily. 'Thanks for coming so early. It's going to be a hot day so it's best if we get cracking.'

The first hurdle she came to was not the lack of co-operation from one-third of her work team but the fact that the ancient-looking lawnmower in the garden shed refused to start.

Ty, who up until this point had been doing nothing more than kicking at the ground with his foot in a surly silence, stepped forward. 'Here, let me have a look. I know a bit about engines.'

Kellie stood back as he set to work tinkering with the old engine. He checked the oil and fuel before he undid the carburetor, cleaning it with a cloth before putting it back together. The engine coughed and choked a couple of times before starting with a splutter.

Kellie grinned at him. 'Wow! That was amazing.'

He gave her an anyone-with-half-a-brain-could-do-it shrug and began to push the mower through the straggly grass.

Kellie inwardly sighed with satisfaction before she turned to the other two boys. 'Stay out of his way, Rowan and Cade, in case anything flies up,' she cautioned. 'There's no catcher on the mower and I don't want any of us to lose an eye or something.'

'What can I do?' Cade asked eagerly.

Kellie smiled as she handed him a rake with two of its teeth missing. 'How about you rake up what you can where Ty's mowed while Rowan and I empty all the dead pots and pull that dead vine off the fence. We'll put all the rubbish in one heap and I'll organise for someone to get rid of it later.'

A couple of hours later there was a pile of rubbish almost as high as Cade. The yard looked a lot neater and although there was still work to be done Kellie didn't want to exhaust the boys to the point where they wouldn't want to come and help again. She brought out ice-cold drinks and some chocolate-chip cookies she'd made the night before, and they sat on the shady side of the veranda out of the heat of the sun.

Rowan and Cade did most of the talking in response to any of the open-ended questions Kellie asked in an effort to build her rapport with them, but Ty remained mostly silent until something caught his eye near the shed.

'Hey, there's that dog that's been hanging around school,' he said, and leapt up to get a pebble to throw at it.

'*No!*' Kellie grabbed him by the arm to stop him. 'Please, don't scare him away. I'm trying to tame him.'

Ty scowled and shrugged off her hand. 'You're wasting your time,' he said, aiming the pebble at a can on the top of the rubbish heap and hitting it with a sharp ping. 'You'll never tame that one. He's totally wild.'

'I think he's frightened, not wild,' Kellie said, watching as the dog peered at them from behind the shed. 'Look at him, he's neglected and filthy.'

'That's because he's been digging,' Rowan said. 'When I was clearing the vine off the fence behind the shed, I saw where he was digging up a bone.'

'A bone?' Kellie asked, as a faint shiver ran up her spine to disturb the hairs at the back of her neck. 'What sort of bone?'

He gave a disinterested shrug. 'I dunno…a bone sort of bone.'

'But I haven't given him any bones,' she said, frowning. 'I've only left out fresh meat and water.'

The three boys exchanged glances.

Ty was the first off the veranda with Rowan close behind. Kellie got there at the same time as Cade and she looked down at the patch of earth where a whitened bone was sticking out of the ground.

Ty bent down but she blocked him with her outstretched arm. 'No,' she said, suppressing a shudder. 'Don't touch it.'

He looked at her as if she was losing her senses. 'What's wrong?' he asked. 'It's just a bone, for God's sake.'

There was a sound from the driveway and a familiar deep voice called out. 'Anyone home?'

Kellie felt such a giant wave of relief flood her she wanted to throw herself into Matt's arms as he came around to where they were standing. The three boys standing there, watching, was the only thing that stopped her, but only just.

'I brought the ute around to take the rubbish away for you,' Matt said. 'Hi, guys,' he addressed the boys. Suddenly noticing the tense atmosphere, he asked, 'What's going on?'

'Rowan found a bone,' Cade piped up. 'Do you think it's human?'

Matt's eyes flicked to Kellie's wide ones. 'Hard to tell,' he said, looking at the specimen for a moment. 'We'd better call the police, though, to make sure.'

'The cops?' Ty and Rowan spoke in unison.

Matt crouched down and examined the bone a little more closely, but refrained from touching it. He knew exactly what sort of bone it was and so did Kellie if the look on her face was anything to go by. But he didn't want the Smithton boys running all over town with the news of a human bone found in the Montgomerys' back yard.

He straightened from the ground and faced the boys. 'It could be someone's Sunday roast, of course, but it's always best to make sure.'

'I've got things to do,' Ty announced cagily.

'Me, too,' Rowan was quick to add.

Cade's eyes were bug-like. 'Do you think there's a dead body buried in Dr Thorne's back yard?' he asked.

Kellie gave a visible shudder.

'Go home, boys,' Matt said firmly. 'Dr Thorne and I will hang around for the police.'

Ty folded his arms in an indomitable pose. 'We're not going until we're paid,' he said.

Kellie brushed the sticky hair out of her eyes. 'I'm so sorry, I almost forgot. I won't be a minute.'

Matt's eyes followed her as she dashed inside the house, returning a short time later and handing each of the boys some notes. They thanked her and left, jostling and nudging each other as they went up the street.

'Are you OK?' Matt asked Kellie once he had called the local sergeant.

She was standing hugging herself as if an arctic breeze was blowing holes into her chest, even though it was close to thirty-eight degrees in the shade. 'I knew there was some-

thing about this house,' she said. 'Properties have person-
alities and this one was giving off spooky signals right from
the word go.'

He didn't answer but stood looking down at the bone.

She gave him a worried look. 'Do you think it might be
Ruth's daughter?'

Matt had tried not to jump to any conclusions but he would
be lying if he didn't admit to thinking the very same thing.
But before the forensic team arrived, which, according to
Greg Blake, the local sergeant could take several hours, it was
probably best for all concerned to keep things low key. He
hated the thought of Ruth being confronted with the possibility that her daughter's body was lying behind the
Montgomerys' shed. It was every parent's nightmare to have
a child go missing but somehow the body-in-the-back-yard
scenario made it even more harrowing and gruesome.

He blew out a sigh and turned away from the grisly object.
'This is not turning out to be great start for you in the bush,'
he commented wryly.

She gave him a weak smile. 'I admit it's not quite what I was
expecting…' she glanced back at the bone '…especially this.'

His gaze swept over the yard. 'You and the boys did a good
job,' he said. 'I'm impressed.'

'Ty was a miracle worker on the mower,' she told him.
'He'd make a great mechanic. He seems to have a natural flair
for that sort of thing.'

'You did both him and Julie a favour, getting him out of
the house for a legitimate purpose,' he said. 'He usually only
goes out to make mischief. I don't think he's been to school
for the past month. He was suspended for a week for some
misdemeanour and hasn't gone back. Julie's been tearing her
hair out over him.'

'He's a nice enough kid,' Kellie said. 'He's just hurting deep inside.'

Matt looked at her. 'You know what your trouble is, Kellie Thorne?' he asked. 'You want to mother everyone. Ty has his own mother, he doesn't need another one.'

'Maybe not, but he definitely needs a friend,' she countered. 'He reminds me of the dog I'm trying to befriend. He comes close and then backs off in case he gets hurt again. Ty is grieving the loss of his dad. The younger ones are too, but Ty has just stepped up on the bridge to manhood. He's fifteen and full of raging hormones. He's suddenly been thrust into being the man of the house but he's not quite ready for it. He's feeling the pressure and he's acting up because deep inside he's just a little boy who's missing his dad.'

Matt had to look away in case she saw how much her insights affected him. He was familiar with the feelings of emotional abandonment, not just from his mother but his father as well. He suddenly realised he had been lonely for most of his life. Madeleine had eased it in the only way she had known how, but it hadn't really been enough.

Kellie had loved and lost and was still in there, defending any cause she could get her hands on. He couldn't help admiring her for it. She was a brave young woman who wasn't the least bit daunted by what life threw up at her.

He knew if he wasn't careful he would be in very great danger of falling for her. Maybe he was well on his way. It certainly felt like it, even though he had been fighting it almost from the start. She was like a battery recharger that had somehow plugged into his body, making it come to life again after being shut down for years. He could feel energy flowing through him, lighting up the shadows of his soul, making him feel as if he could live again, and fully at that.

It seemed like an hour but it was only a few minutes before Sergeant Greg Blake arrived with a constable called Tracey Chugg.

'The local coroner's been contacted and the forensic pathologist is on his way,' Greg said. 'Fortunately they were working on a case in Roma. They're flying in shortly.'

Kellie stood back and watched as the scene was protected from further contamination. The area was taped off with crime-scene tape and once the forensic team arrived she was kept busy providing cool drinks as the temperature had soared. The humidity in the air was almost unbearable and when she looked up she could see the clustering of dark, brooding clouds that heralded a storm.

Matt came to stand beside her and looked up at the bruised-looking sky. 'We might get some rain out of this,' he said. 'It certainly feels like it.'

There was a sound of rushed footsteps behind them and as Kellie turned she saw Ruth coming towards them, her face twisted in anguish. 'Is it my baby?' she sobbed brokenly. 'Don't tell me it's Tegan.'

Matt enfolded her in a comforting hug, stroking her while looking over her head to Kellie's empathetic gaze. 'Nothing is certain, Ruth,' he said gently. 'It will take a while to find out how old it is or if the bone is male or female.'

Ruth pulled out of his embrace and scrubbed at her face with her hands. 'For all these years I've felt she was still *alive*. I've know it in *here*.' She thumped at her chest where her heart was. 'I don't want her to be dead. Oh, dear God I don't want her to be dead and buried like a bit of rubbish in someone's back yard…'

Kellie put her hand on the older woman's shaking shoulder. 'The police are doing everything they can to establish who this is,' she said. 'They'll let you know as soon as they find out anything.'

Kellie watched as Matt led Ruth away, his strong arms encircling the older woman's shoulders as he spoke to her in soothing tones. Trish arrived and, after exchanging a few words with Matt, took Ruth to her house out of the way of the police and forensic services team.

Tracey, the constable, came to stand beside Kellie. 'I hear you're new in town,' she said. 'Nice way to start a locum, finding a body in your back yard.'

'Is that what this is?' Kellie asked, sneaking a look around the taped-off area. 'It's not just a humerus in there?'

Tracey nodded grimly. 'Whoever put that body there did so in hurry—it's barely two feet under.'

'Is it male or female?' Kellie asked.

'Can't tell yet,' Tracey said. 'We'll have to send the remains to a forensic anthropologist. He or she will be able to establish what age, race and gender the deceased is. Depending on the state of the remains they can sometimes even establish the cause of death.'

Kellie rubbed at her upper arms in spite of the searing temperature. 'I don't think I can stay here another night,' she said. 'I'm not normally such a wimp but this goes way beyond my comfort zone.'

'You won't have to,' Tracey said. 'The local guys will secure and guard the site until everything is assessed. Is there anyone you can spend a couple of nights with until things are formally cleared up here?'

'She can stay with me,' Matt said as he came up behind them after seeing Ruth off with Trish. 'I have a spare room—a couple of rooms, actually.'

Kellie swung around to face him. 'You don't have to do that,' she said, feeling her colour start to rise in her cheeks.

'It's fine,' he said. 'I have plenty of room.'

'But what about the dog?'

'What dog?' Tracey asked, looking confused.

Kellie turned to the constable. 'I've been trying to tame a stray dog,' she explained. 'I've been leaving food out each night but so far he isn't coming close enough for me to approach him.'

'Is that the one that has been lurking around the school lately?' Tracey asked.

'I think so,' Kellie said. 'It looks very thin and scared.'

'We can get rid of it for you if you'd like,' the constable offered matter-of-factly.

Kellie stared at her. 'You mean…get rid of it as in *shoot* it?'

Tracey gave an indifferent shrug. 'If it's causing you any bother then we can do something about it. There's no dog catcher out here, Dr Thorne. If the dog is being a menace, we have the means to remove it.'

Kellie pulled herself up to her full height, which still left her an inch or two short of the formidable constable. 'No, thank you,' she said crisply. 'The dog isn't being a nuisance to me. I don't want it destroyed or removed from this property.'

'The dog isn't a problem, Tracey,' Matt said to the police officer. 'Now that it's being regularly fed by Dr Thorne, I don't think it will be causing any problems at the school. We'll make sure it's fed each day until you guys think it's OK for Kellie to move back into the house.'

Greg Blake joined them at that moment. He asked Kellie a few questions before turning to Matt. 'The Montgomerys have only been away, what, three weeks?'

'Closer to four,' Matt answered. 'Dr Thorne's been in the house about ten days.'

Greg Blake closed his notebook. 'We'll be in touch as soon as we know anything. I'd better go and chat to Ruth. This will hit her hard.'

'You think it's Tegan Williams buried there?' Matt asked, frowning heavily.

'We won't know until the forensic anthropologist dates the remains,' Greg said. 'But I would say that whoever it is buried there has been there for quite some time, at least ten or fifteen years, maybe even more.'

CHAPTER FIFTEEN

'POOR Ruth,' Kellie said later that evening once she was settled in at Matt's house. 'I can't imagine what she must be going through right now.'

Matt handed her a glass of white wine and a bowl of crisps before sitting on the sofa opposite. 'I spoke to Trish earlier,' he said. 'She finally managed to persuade Ruth to take a couple of the sedatives I prescribed and she's now sleeping.'

Kellie suppressed another shudder at the thought of the forensic team digging up the rest of the body. She knew it would be a painstaking task as vital clues could be lost if anything was handled incautiously.

'It might not be her,' Matt said into the silence. 'It might be someone else entirely.'

Kellie ran the tip of her tongue over the dryness of her lips. 'Have there been any other missing persons reported from around here over the last ten or twenty years?'

'Thousands of people go missing every year from all over the country,' he answered. 'It's one of the most frustrating tasks for police trying to track a person's last movements. And then, of course, there are some people don't who just don't want to be found. I read about a guy who ran away from home when he was a teenager. He made no contact whatsoever. His parents subsequently died, never knowing what had happened to their son. By sheer chance his younger sister tracked him down thirty years later living in another country. It turned out he'd had a furious row with his parents over a curfew and took off. He was too proud to come home and apologise.'

'Too proud?' Kellie gaped at him. 'But that's dreadful! Can you imagine what his family went through for all those years? How could he have been so selfish?'

Matt lifted one shoulder in a shrug. 'You know what kids are like at that age,' he said. 'They tend to see things in black and white.'

'Yes, I guess so,' she said. 'I can remember plenty of slammed doors and shouts of "I'm never coming back" at my house too. But fortunately everyone came back…' She snagged her bottom lip momentarily. 'Except my mother, of course….'

Matt saw the flicker of grief pass over her features and, putting down his glass, got up and joined her on the other sofa. He put his arm around her shoulders and gently squeezed. 'You did a great job with those boys today,' he said. 'It was a shame the day had to end the way it did, but you showed an interest in them few others have done. Ty, for instance. I had no idea he was interested in all things mechanical and I've lived here for six years. You've been here ten days or so and you've already got everyone eating out of your hand.'

She turned her head to look into his eyes, her toffee-brown gaze luminous. 'Not quite everyone,' she said softly.

Matt looked at the tiny dusting of salt on her lips from the crisps she had nibbled on and felt his groin instantly surge with blood. He wanted to taste every salty inch of her, he wanted to feel her softness against his hardness, to explore the curves of her body that he knew instinctively would align perfectly with his. The desire to do so was like a hot river of need racing beneath his skin; he could feel it pumping him to erectness, the ache for fulfilment so overwhelming he knew it would take all his self-control and more to stop himself from sealing her mouth with his.

'You've got salt on your lips,' he said, his voice coming out far too husky.

'Have I?' Her tongue basted her lips. 'All gone?'

His gaze locked on her mouth. 'Er…not quite.'

She did another circuit of her lips with the point of her tongue. 'What about now?'

'There's a tiny bit there,' he said pointing to the lower curve of her bottom lip.

Her tongue came out before he could move away and brushed against his fingertip. It was the most erotic thing he had ever experienced. It sent lightning bolts of electricity to every part of his body. His skin burned with the heat of her touch, and before he had any hope of restraining himself he brought his mouth crashing down on hers.

It was a kiss of pent-up passion, long-denied needs and mutual longing. He could feel her frustration mingling with his in a combustible impact that left no part of him unaffected. His body was out of control, riding a wave of desire so fast and furious he had no hope of keeping his head. He wanted more of her; he wanted to bury himself in her softness, to drive himself to oblivion.

Kellie gasped in delight as his tongue drove through the soft shield of her lips and found hers, tangling with it, taming it in a duel-like dance that signified his ultimate intent. She could feel the hard swell of his erection as he pressed her back down on the sofa, his body a blessed weight on the floating neediness of hers. His thighs bracketed hers, but as his kiss intensified he deftly nudged them apart, settling between them with the full force of his masculinity.

Her body ached and pulsed with need. She arched her back with a wantonness that was totally unfamiliar to her. She had never experienced such an avalanche of emotion before. The twin fires of love and lust burned in the cauldron of her body, each vying for supremacy.

Love? Kellie felt herself take a momentary mental back step. Was that what was happening to her? It felt so right being in his arms like this, with his body responding to hers with such urgency and purpose, as if he had waited all this time for her to come along.

When his hands scooped beneath her top and bra and found her breasts, Kellie's whole body shivered in reaction. His palms flattened her, shaped her and moulded her before he bent his head and anointed her with the hot moist cave of his mouth. Her nipples were so tight each stroke of his tongue was exquisite torture, making her squirm beneath him for more of his masterful touch. How on earth had she lived this long without this passionate madness? she wondered as his teeth scraped erotically against her sensitive flesh.

Her body was suddenly a stranger to her; she barely recognised the responses she could feel raging through her. Each nerve had come to fizzing life, dancing and leaping beneath her skin. It seemed like each and every part of her was becoming more and more impatient for his touch.

Her stomach almost caved in with need when he pulled on her bottom lip with his teeth, the sexy movement of his lips and tongue sending her spinning out of control. The stubble on his jaw scraped at the softer skin of her face as he angled his head to deepen the kiss even further, sending her pulse right off the scale.

She tugged his shirt out of his trousers and explored his naked chest with her hands, relishing the feel of hard muscles and the light dusting of hair. She let her fingers move lower, following the trail of hair that went below his waistband, her fingers fumbling with the fastening for a moment before she finally freed him into the soft, worshipful caress of her hands.

He was so very aroused she could smell it on his skin, the musk and salt and urgency a potent combination, sending her senses into overdrive. She had seen a lot of male bodies but none had ever taken her breath away quite like his. Everything about him was perfect; each contour of his body was toned and leanly muscled. The satin strength and the thickness of him that indicated how much she had affected him made her feel utterly feminine and complete in a way she had never felt before.

She wriggled down so she could taste him, the act one she had never felt comfortable with before, but somehow this time it felt so natural, so in tune with what she felt for him she didn't hesitate for a moment. She felt him jerk against her in response, his harshly indrawn breath a clue to how close he was to losing control, but she continued to use her lips and tongue.

Matt suddenly pulled away from her, avoiding her eyes, avoiding further contact and most especially avoiding the mantelpiece where the green watchful gaze of his dead fiancée seemed to be trained on him accusingly. 'I'm sorry,' he said, zipping himself back into place. 'That wasn't meant to happen. In fact, I can't believe it just did.'

Kellie looked at him in bewilderment, her senses knocked off course by his abrupt rejection. She couldn't speak for the emotion clogging her throat. She had thought he had been with her all the way. Was she so naïve and inexperienced that she had totally misread him? Shame flooded her. She felt so exposed and vulnerable she could barely look at him without flinching.

He turned to face her, his expression criss-crossed with a frown. 'It shouldn't have happened, Kellie. You know it shouldn't. We're colleagues who have to work together for six months. It doesn't mean we have to sleep together. It's not written into the contract.'

'But…but you kissed me…' Kellie moistened her still sensitive mouth and continued in the same confused tone, 'I thought you were…you know…developing feelings for me…' She bit her bottom lip until she could feel it swelling around her teeth. 'I've never felt like this before…with anyone… It feels so right. I thought you were starting to feel the same way… Your kiss seemed to indicate…'

He scraped a hand through his hair as he stepped away. 'You can't possibly fall in love with me,' he said, hardly game to believe it was possible. She was an impulsive young woman, caught up in the heat of the moment, no doubt feeling guilty she had become so intimate with him in so short a time. In a few days she would see this episode in a new light. It was up to him to give her an out. It was the gentlemanly thing to do. She had been cruelly hurt before. She needed more time to get to know him before anything between them was established.

'It's her, isn't it?' she asked into the tight silence.

He clenched his shadowed jaw. 'Don't do this, Kellie,' he bit out. 'Don't make this any harder than it is.'

She got to her feet and, moving across to the mantelpiece, turned the photograph of Madeleine around. 'There,' she said stridently. 'Are you available now?'

He glared at her in anger, his hands going to fists by his sides. 'This is not about her, damn you.'

She came up to him and jabbed him in the chest with the point of her index finger. 'You are *alive*, Matt, she is dead.

D-E-A-D. You can't change that. The only thing you can change is how you live your life now.'

He pushed her hand away. 'I don't want this. I don't need the complication of this right now. And if you were honest with yourself, neither do you.'

'Yes, you *do* want this!' she cried. 'You would never have reacted the way you did unless—'

'So where were you on the day they taught male sexual response at medical school?' he said cuttingly. 'Anyone could have achieved the same result you just did. It has nothing to do with feelings and emotions, it's totally physical.'

Kellie swung away, her pride so tattered and torn she felt sick to her stomach. 'I'm s-sorry,' she said, hoping he wouldn't hear the catch in her voice. 'I obviously completely misread the situation. Put it down to my appalling lack of experience…or something…'

A little silence pulsed in the air for a moment.

'Forget about it,' he said gently. 'We were both caught out by today's drama. Emotions can often get out of hand in tense situations.'

She moved towards the sitting-room door, her back turned towards him. 'I think I'll give dinner a miss if you don't mind,' she said. 'I'm very tired. I'm often irrational when I'm overtired.'

'It wasn't your fault, Kellie,' he said. 'If anyone is to blame, it's me. I started it with that kiss. I'm sorry. I stepped way over the line. It's no wonder you jumped to the conclusions you did. Any woman would have done so.'

She turned back to look at him briefly. 'You have to let her go, Matt,' she said softly. 'Some day, some time you have to finally let her go.'

Matt watched her leave the room, his body still on fire, his

heart torn between wanting to go after her and claim her as his own and the other part of him wanting to go over to the mantelpiece and turn Madeleine's photograph back to face the room and his conscience.

In the end he drained the contents of his wineglass and left Madeleine facing the wall—he kind of felt she had seen enough for one day.

Kellie was up early next morning in an effort to avoid running into Matt, but she needn't have bothered as he was nowhere in sight. On her way into town she drove past the Montgomerys' house but it was still cordoned off so she carried on to the clinic instead.

'How is Ruth?' she asked Trish, who was already sitting at the reception desk.

'Matt's spending some time with her now,' Trish said. 'She's terribly upset, as you can imagine.'

'Have the police established anything yet?' Kellie asked.

'Not yet. The forensic team is still at the site.'

'Yes, I saw them as I drove past,' Kellie said, trying not to shiver in reaction. 'I used to have such a normal, boring life.'

'You'd better give your family a call to let them know what's going on,' Trish suggested, handing her the newspaper. 'They might find it a little disturbing to hear about it in the press.'

'I called my father late last night,' Kellie said relieved she had done so now that she had seen the headlines. 'He wants me to come straight home.'

'You're not going to, are you?' Trish looked worried.

She blew out a sigh and put the newspaper down. 'No. I made a commitment and I'm determined to see it through.' *Even if I have made the biggest fool out of myself*, Kellie thought.

'So…' Trish gave her a penetrating glance. 'How are you getting on with Matt? I heard you spent the night at his place last night.'

Kellie shifted her gaze to look at the list of patients. 'We're getting on just fine. He's very professional at all times.'

'He's certainly been very supportive of you with the mothers' group project,' Trish observed. 'He's been working the most ungodly hours to see that everything you want gets done.'

'I know what you're thinking, Trish, but it's not going to happen,' Kellie said. 'He's a nice guy and all that but he's in love with a dead woman. I can't compete with that. I don't want to even try.'

'I think you're in with a very good chance. You're the first woman he's shown any interest in whatsoever. I see the way he looks at you. He's never looked at anyone like that before.'

'I think it would be better if everyone left him alone,' Kellie grumbled. 'Besides, who said I was interested in him?'

Trish gave her a knowing look. 'Come on, Kellie, you have one of the most expressive faces this town has ever seen,' she said. 'I know you got off to a rocky start with him but it's obvious as those cute little freckles on the bridge of your nose that you're falling in love with him. In fact, I'd hazard a guess you already *are* a little bit in love with him. I can see it in your eyes. You practically melt whenever his name is mentioned.'

'That's ridiculous.' Kellie attempted to deny it but she knew her colour was probably giving her away. 'What sort of crazy person would fall in love with someone after just a few days? That stuff only happens in movies and paperback novels. Anyway, I didn't come out here to find myself a husband, and if I had Matt McNaught is definitely not husband material. He's married to his memories.'

'People do sometimes fall in love within days, if not

minutes,' Trish countered. 'I fell in love with my husband the moment I met him, I just had to wait for a couple of dates for him to catch up. And as for Matt and his memories, I don't think it will take him too long to realise what's landed right under his nose. In any case, I can't remember the last time he mentioned his late fiancée. I get the feeling he's well and truly ready to move on. The whole town thinks so, too. Nothing would please everyone more than seeing him settle down with someone like you. You've brought life and vigour to this dry old town.'

The first patient arrived, which put an end to the exchange, for which Kellie was rather thankful. She hadn't realised her feelings were so obvious but, then, just thinking about what had happened between her and Matt last night was enough to make her whole body light up with the glow of guilt and shame.

She still couldn't quite believe she had been so bold and brazen. She mentally cringed in embarrassment. She had practically seduced him. No, she *had* seduced him! There was no point pretending otherwise. She had responded to him in such a manner uncharacteristic of her upbringing, out of line with her beliefs and moral standards.

What on earth had she been thinking? Sex didn't equal love. He had told her so himself. He had at least had the decency and sense to call a halt before things had got even further out of hand.

She of all people knew the dangers of casual sex. She had seen enough patients with sexually transmitted diseases to know how risky it was, and yet if he hadn't pulled back she would have been his for the asking. He had gallantly taken some of the blame for kissing her, but where had her self-control been when she'd needed it? Being someone's sex buddy was definitely not in her scheme of things. She wanted marriage and babies and the whole shebang—the white wedding and the honeymoon in paradise. She had dreamed of it since she was a little girl. She had tottered around the house in her mother's high heels, her entire body consumed by the slightly yellowed wedding veil, conjuring up her very own Mr Right. He wasn't supposed to come with baggage. He was supposed to love her and only her. How could she settle for anything less?

Kellie picked up the first patient's file and plastered a smile on her face. 'Mrs Overton?'

Pat Overton was a frail woman in her sixties who had been battling breast cancer for the last five years. Kellie knew from the notes that things did not look promising. Despite a mastectomy with axillary clearance and adjuvant tamoxifen, the cancer had metastasised to the lungs, pleura and thoracic spine. She had refused to go to Brisbane for radiotherapy to the bony involvement—she didn't want to be away from the countryside for even one day and she had already been changed to arimidex, but with no obvious improvement. She had also refused chemotherapy.

Kellie's examination showed a large left pleural effusion and crepitations over most of both lungs. The thoracic spine and some of the ribs were very tender.

It was a levelling moment, to be sitting so close to someone who was so close to death and who obviously knew it. Kellie could see the sad resignation in the older woman's grey-blue eyes and her heart ached for what her family would be going through right now and in the few short weeks ahead.

'I'm so tired of fighting,' Pat said breathlessly. 'I've come to the end of my rope. I've managed on the painkillers Dr Montgomery gave me before he left but I think it's time for something stronger. I was going to see Dr McNaught but I thought it might be nice to meet you. I'd heard you were quite lovely and I can see now it's true.'

'That's very sweet of you but I—'

'He's a good man, Dr Thorne.'

'Yes, I know, he's—'

'He'll make someone a wonderful husband one day.' Pat had cut her off again.

'I'm sure he will. However—'

Pat grasped her by the hand. 'My husband will do the same, I know it. We've been together a long time but that doesn't mean he can't find happiness and companionship with someone else after I've gone. I've tried to tell him but he won't listen. Men can be so stubborn, don't you think?'

Kellie swallowed the lump of emotion in her throat. 'Yes,' she said, 'exasperatingly so.'

Pat smiled and sat back with a sigh. 'Now, give me something to knock the back teeth out of this pain and I'll leave you to get on with your young life. I've had mine and it's been a good one. I've brought up two sons and two daughters and I've had the privilege of being a grandmother six times. I wish I could stay around for the rest but that's not God's plan.'

'I can escalate the pain relief a lot,' Kellie said, discreetly clearing her throat as she reached for the prescription pad. 'I'm going to start you on a medium dose of long-acting morphine. That will ease the breathlessness a little too. We'll up the dose until you feel comfortable.'

'Thank you, Dr Thorne,' Pat said. Reaching out, she touched Kellie softly on the arm, her pain-filled eyes meeting hers. 'Thank you for caring so much.'

Kellie blinked back tears. 'I can't help it, Mrs Overton,' she said.

The older woman smiled. 'Yes, I can see that. It's what everyone loves about you. Even Matt McNaught.'

CHAPTER SIXTEEN

MATT was in the staff kitchen when Kellie came in, blowing her nose. He looked up from the newspaper and frowned. 'Are you all right?'

She nodded and stuffed the tissue into her bra. 'I've just spent over an hour with Pat Overton.'

'Oh.' His one-word response summed it up completely.

Kellie plucked another tissue out of the box on the counter and buried her reddened nose into it. 'She's so brave and so selfless, it really got to me.'

'She has been very brave about it all,' he agreed. 'Tim and I have often spoken about her courage. She's put up an incredible fight.'

'Why does it happen to such nice people?' she asked looking up at him through tear-washed eyes. 'Why do such lovely people get struck down when there are horrible murderers and rapists on the loose?'

Matt let out a sigh and came over to where she was standing, snivelling into another scrunched-up tissue. He had told himself after last night he wasn't going to touch her again. He had practically drawn an invisible line around her body as a no-go area. But somehow she had this weird effect on him—it was like he was a tiny iron filing and she was a super-sized magnet.

'It happens because life is sometimes totally unfair,' he said, breathing in the sweet scent of her as she nestled against him. 'I don't have any answers, Kellie. I'm the one still asking the unanswerable questions.'

'Pat is worried about her husband,' she said stepping out of his embrace. 'She wants him to move on after she's gone. I wish my mother had said that to my father. I think it would have made it easier for him.'

Matt shoved his hands in his trouser pockets to keep them away from where they really wanted to go. 'It's a personal thing,' he said. 'No one can put a time limit on it. Joe Overton will have to work through it for himself. He and Pat have been together a long time. They've raised a family together and watched their farm go through all the highs and lows of droughts and floods and good years. He will miss her dreadfully when she goes, but at least he's had some warning.'

She pulled out another tissue and wiped at her eyes. 'Do you think that makes it easier?' she asked.

His chest deflated on a sigh. 'I don't know. What do you think? You've been in practice long enough to have seen just about everything there is to be seen. Do you think it makes a difference?'

'I'm not sure…' She chewed at her bottom lip in that little-girl-lost sort of way that did twisting and turning things to his insides every single time. 'I think it varies from person to person. Some people cope really well with the sudden death of a relative, others have trouble coping with watching a loved one go through the process of a drawn-out terminal illness.'

'If Pat Overton is a little too close personally, I'll take over her care for you,' he offered.

She looked up at him, her eyes still red and glistening with tears. 'No. I want to look after her. I want to do whatever I can for her and her family.'

A silence began to shrink the size of the room.

'About last night…' he began awkwardly.

'No,' she said, squeezing her eyes shut and holding up a hand to stall him. '*Please*, don't make me suffer any more embarrassment than I already have. I can't believe I was so…so…out of control. I've never done that…you know… I mean, I've read about it in all those modern women's magazines but I've never actually…well…you know…taken it to that point…'

'Don't worry about it,' he said. 'I told you it wasn't entirely your fault. I could easily have stopped things before they got to that point…' He twisted his mouth ruefully. 'Well, maybe not easily, but I should have all the same.'

Her gaze dropped away from his. 'I'm sorry,' she said. 'I can't imagine what you must be thinking of me. I'm normally the biggest prude out. For years I've been plugging up my ears when my brothers start talking about their sex lives. I just don't want to know what they get up to or who with.'

'It's another one of those personal things,' he said. 'What feels right for one person isn't right for another.'

'I hope I haven't compromised our working relationship,' she said, starting to gnaw at her lip again.

'It's fine, Kellie, really,' he said. 'It was an unusual day. It's not every day you find a skeleton in your back yard. It's no wonder we were both a little out of kilter.' He took a breath and mentally rehearsed what he had really wanted to say but just as he opened his mouth Trish came in.

'Oh, sorry,' she said, with one of her knowing smiles. 'I was just wondering if I could get you two a cup of tea or something?'

Matt silently ground his teeth behind his polite smile. 'No, thank you, Trish,' he said. 'I have a house call to make out at the Fairworth property. I should have left ten minutes ago.'

'How is Ruth managing?' Trish asked.

'She's trying to be strong but it's knocking her around,' he said. 'It will be a huge blow to her if it turns out to be Tegan. She has kept herself going for so long on the hope that her daughter is still alive. I'm really worried about how she will deal with it if the worst comes to pass.'

'I can't imagine the hell Ruth is going through,' Kellie said once Trish had bustled out to answer the phone. 'It must be so hard to keep on hoping when there is really no hope.'

Matt picked up a card and handed it to her. 'I thought you might like to see this,' he said. 'It's from Brayden Harrison. He's out of the induced coma and doing really well. He particularly wanted to thank you after he heard you had been on a run and got waylaid by his injuries.'

Kellie read the card and felt her eyes water again. 'Wow,' she said, tucking the card back into the envelope. 'It makes me glad I chose to be a doctor instead of an orthodontist.'

He gave her a wry smile. 'An orthodontist?'

She nodded. 'It was the braces I had when I was a teenager. I toyed with the idea for a while but then I realised I had another calling.'

'You're a damned good doctor, Kellie,' he said. 'I'm not sure Brayden would be alive today if you hadn't been there with me that day.'

Another silence brought the walls closer together.

'I have to get back to work,' she said, turning away. 'Gracie Young's middle child has an ear infection. I think I can hear her crying in the waiting room. I've squeezed her in between Mr Tate and Mrs Peters.'

'Kellie, wait,' Matt said, hoping Jean Fairworth and her migraine would forgive him another minute or two.

Kellie turned back to look at him. 'Yes?'

His throat moved up and down in a tight swallow. 'I just wanted to say if you want to leave, that would be fine with me. It's not been a pleasant experience so far and I thought if you wanted to pack it in before the six months is up, I wouldn't make a fuss about it. It might take some time but we can find someone else.'

She frowned at him. 'You *want* me to leave? Is that what you're saying?'

Matt felt like kicking himself. What was wrong with him? Why had he said that? Of course he didn't want her to leave. She was an asset to the place. No, she was much more than that. She was the most beautiful, adorable, dimple-cheeked woman he'd ever met and he wanted to spend the rest of his days telling her how much she had come to mean to him. He scraped a hand through his hair and tried again. 'No, that's not what I'm saying, not really.'

'Then what are you saying, Matt?' she asked with a look that would have sent a raging bull ten paces backwards.

He cleared his throat. 'Look, I'm just trying to make things easier for everyone.'

Her brown eyes flashed with sparks of resentment. 'For yourself, you mean. What's worrying you, Matt? That word might somehow get out in town that you allowed yourself to be human for change? That you have needs and desires and urges, just like everyone else?'

He frowned back at her, annoyed with how he had bungled things and equally annoyed at her for not giving him a chance to explain himself. 'You were appointed to this position as a fellow GP, not as a solution to my lack of a love life,' he clipped out. 'I suggest you get on with the tasks assigned you as part of your contract and leave me to deal with my own issues in my own time.'

Kellie's mouth tightened so much her jaw ached. 'You're never going to deal with any of those issues, Matt, because you're an emotional coward. You've never forgiven your mother for leaving you and your father, just like you've never forgiven Madeleine for dying. That's your problem, you know. You're angry at her for getting killed but you can't admit it so you wear your hairshirt way out here in the sticks, making everyone feel sorry for you. It's pathetic, that's what it is—totally pathetic.'

He glared at her in fury. 'I think you might have said quite enough, Dr Thorne,' he bit out. 'I also think you might want to have a rethink about returning to the city where you and your psychology belong. There's no place for it here.'

Kellie pulled back her shoulders as he stalked past, her chest heaving with anger as he left the room with the victory of the last word ringing in her ears.

The police were just leaving the Montgomerys' house when Kellie called in after work. She was assured that everything was fine for her to resume living in the house; they had finally removed the remains and were now waiting for confirmation of the identity of the deceased.

Kellie left some food out in case the stray dog was about before making her way around to Ruth Williams's house. Trish had informed her earlier that afternoon that Ruth had insisted on returning home to wait for the police to contact her.

When Ruth answered the door to Kellie's knock it was clear the waiting was taking its toll. Her face was sunken with anguish, the conflicting lines of grief and hope like a complicated map written on her forehead.

'Oh, Kellie, my dear,' she said, sinking into Kellie's embrace. 'How did you know I needed some company right now?'

'Have you heard anything?' Kellie asked once they were seated in the sitting room.

Ruth shook her head. 'Sergeant Blake said he would call me as soon as he finds out who it is.' She glanced at the phone by her right side and added wearily, 'I hope it won't be too much longer now…'

Kellie's gaze went to a sideboard, where an array of photographs was displayed. 'Is that Tegan?' she asked.

Ruth nodded sadly. 'Yes, that's my girl.'

'She was very beautiful,' Kellie said, and then wondered if she should have used the past tense.

'Yes,' Ruth said with a sad smile. 'She used to love posing for the camera. She loved being the centre of attention, she craved it. I guess that's why she and Dirk clashed so much. She wasn't used to sharing me with anyone after her father died.'

'Is this Dirk?' Kellie asked, picking up a photograph of a sandy-haired man with an open easy smile.

Ruth let out a sigh. 'No, that's my first husband, Tegan's father Alan. Dirk never used to like me having Alan's photo there, but when he passed away I put Alan back.'

Kellie's eyes scanned the rest of the display. 'Do you have any photos of your second husband?'

'Not now,' Ruth answered. 'I sent them to his parents after he died. I didn't really want them any more, to tell you the truth. Alan was my first love. Tegan was right, she told me often enough before she…left. I should never have tried to replace him.'

Kellie swallowed as the older woman's gaze centred on hers. She felt Ruth could see every emotion she was feeling as if they were individually etched on her skin—her escalating feelings for Matt, how she loved him and wanted him to take that step away from the past towards her open arms.

'You will have to be patient, Kellie,' Ruth said with a tender look. 'From the little he's told me, I know Matt's whole life and future was built around Madeleine. She represented the security he had been lacking all his life. Her shock death was like suddenly turning a corner and slamming into an invisible brick wall. He was planning his wedding one day, the next he was organising her funeral. He didn't see it coming, no one does. But he will heal in time—I can already see signs of it. Maybe he feels he can't quite let go just yet because in doing so he will have to finally accept he has lost her for ever. That's the hardest part, realising the one you love isn't coming back.'

Kellie pressed her lips together as the tears started to flow. 'I just want him to make some room in his heart for me,' she said. 'Is that asking too much? I've waited all my adult life to meet someone who makes me feel like this, only to find his emotions are tied up elsewhere. How can I ever be the one he wants when the one he really wants is dead?'

Ruth reached for her hands and held them in the soft warmth of hers. 'Listen to me, Kellie,' she commanded gently. 'You're a beautiful, caring person. Anyone can see that. I saw it the moment you stepped off that plane. I think Matt *is* starting to see what he's missing out on. He's isolated himself out here like a wounded lonely wolf to brood and lick his wounds in private. For six long years he's punished himself for not being able to keep Madeleine safe from the vicissitudes of life.

'But the fact is it's not possible to keep *anyone* we love safe. We have to accept that and live the life we've been given. I've come to realise over the years that life isn't a dress rehearsal—it's actually a one-act play.' Ruth sat back, sighing deeply as she continued, 'I miss my daughter, every day I ache for the years I've lost with her, but I have to press on. Whatever the outcome of the forensic investigation, I have come to realise there are other people in this community who need me. I draw strength from that. It's what keeps me going, it's what has always kept me going.'

Kellie brushed at her eyes with the back of her hand. 'You remind me of my mother,' she said. 'I think if one of my brothers or I had gone missing, she would have been the same as you, waiting indefinitely. She would never have given up hope, not until the evidence was before her to convince her otherwise.'

'There are so many different types of grief, Kellie,' Ruth said. 'Look at Trish and David Cutler, for example. All they ever wanted to do was get married and have babies, but it wasn't to be. The irony is that nowadays they may well have achieved it with a couple of IVF attempts, but that wasn't available then. They were told to go away and forget about it or apply for adoption, but by the time they got around to doing it they were considered too old so they missed out. Life is full of disappointments, though, isn't it? No doubt you've been a doctor long enough now to realise how unfair it all is.'

'Yes, it certainly is,' Kellie agreed, thinking of the lovely and incredibly courageous Pat Overton.

There was a knock at the door and Kellie offered to answer it. 'Thank you, dear,' Ruth said. 'I've been up and down all day. It's probably Julie—she said she'd call around about now.'

Kellie came back into the sitting room with Greg and Tracey. 'It's the police,' she said, unconsciously holding her breath. 'They have some news for you.'

CHAPTER SEVENTEEN

'HAVE you heard the news?' Cheryl asked Matt when he came to the general store to pick up a special item he had ordered.

'No,' he said, trying to gauge her expression. 'Is it about Tegan Williams?'

'Apparently it's not her,' Cheryl said. 'It wasn't her body buried at the Montgomerys' house. The police have now identified it's a man.'

'Who was he?' Matt asked, frowning.

'Apparently he was an international tourist on a working holiday who came through twenty-five years or so ago,' Cheryl reported. 'The Montgomerys' house used to be a bit of a backpackers' cottage back then. It was a pretty ad hoc arrangement, I seem to recall. I don't think anyone paid much for staying there as it was pretty rundown. Anyway, he was travelling with three friends from Europe, picking up work when and where they could. They didn't stay in town long, a couple of days at the most.'

'So how did he come to be buried in the back yard?' Matt asked.

'Well, it seems after a solid night of heavy drinking, the guys all bunked down to sleep, but during the night one of them vomited and choked to death. When the other two found him dead the next morning they panicked. They felt responsible because they had been the ones to encourage him to drink shot after shot of vodka. They didn't speak much English and were worried they would be charged with manslaughter or something.'

'So they just *buried* him behind the shed and left town?' Matt asked with an incredulous expression.

'Yep,' Cheryl said. 'The federal police finally tracked the two guys down on the basis of the dead man's dental records. There's an international database on missing persons so they were able to find his travelling companions. They told the police everything. Imagine living with that on your conscience for all these years? Hard on the dead guy's family after all this time, but at least now they've got closure. His remains will be sent back for a proper burial. The authorities are seeing to it as we speak.'

'I'd better go and see Ruth,' Matt said, running a hand through his hair. 'She's been to hell and back and she still has no answers.'

'Kellie was with her earlier,' Cheryl said. 'I heard our pretty young doctor spent the night with you. Counting the one in Brisbane, that's two nights you've spent with her so far. So what's going on with you two?'

Matt's brows moved together. 'What do you mean?'

Cheryl's eyes glinted. 'Come on, Matt, what are you waiting for? She's everything a man could want. You'd be a fool to let her slip through your fingers. If you don't snap her up someone else will, and then what will you do? Spend the rest of your life out here sulking about yet another one that got away?'

He picked up his items from the counter, his mouth pulled tight. 'Put it on the tab, Cheryl,' he bit out as he strode out of the store.

* * *

Kellie didn't see much of Matt over the next few days. Apparently there had been a mechanical problem with the plane on one of the outback clinic runs, which had meant he and the pilot had had to stay at one of the grazing properties until it was fixed.

Matt had called her one evening but his conversation had seemed rather stilted so she'd decided to make up an excuse about having to wash her hair. The fact that he hadn't even questioned her rather hackneyed excuse had seemed to suggest he'd been relieved she'd brought an end to an already uncomfortable conversation.

The clinic in town took up as much time as Kellie had available and with her extra commitments at the community centre she was glad she didn't have too much time on her hands to think about Matt.

Kellie was more than delighted at how well the young mothers were getting on. She had conducted several cooking classes with Ruth's help and the girls themselves had come up with the brilliant suggestion of planning a charity dinner prepared by them to raise funds for Christmas presents for the underprivileged kids in town.

A few evenings later, once Matt had got safely back from the regional clinic, his manager Bob Gardner and his wife Eunice invited her out for a meal at their cottage.

Kellie accepted the invitation with enthusiasm, as even though her days at the clinic and the community centre were long, the nights at the Montgomerys' were even longer. Although she had to admit her enthusiasm underwent a quick change once Eunice informed her Matt would be joining them for dinner.

It seemed from the moment Kellie was welcomed effusively in the door by Bob and Eunice, Matt not only evaded addressing a word to her but seemed to be avoiding even looking at her.

Bob was called away to the phone at one point and Eunice bustled out, mumbling something about seeing to the apple crumble in the oven, which left Kellie alone with Matt at the dining table.

The silence was almost palpable.

'Ruth seems to have recovered well,' he finally said, still looking at the contents of his wineglass.

'Yes,' Kellie responded. 'She's been a great help to me with the mothers' group.' She briefly filled him in on the charity dinner the girls had planned, and for her trouble got a mono-syllabic reply.

Another silence passed.

Matt cleared his throat and met her gaze across the table. 'Kellie…I was wondering if we could get together some time to—'

Eunice came in at that point with a fresh jug of iced water. 'Did Dr Thorne tell you about the young mothers' charity dinner?' she asked.

Matt forced himself to smile. 'Yes, it sounds like a great idea.'

Eunice put the jiggling-with-ice jug on the table next to Matt. 'I think it's wonderful what Dr Thorne has done in the short time she's been here, don't you?'

'Yes,' Matt said. Picking up the jug, he concentrated on re-filling everyone's glass.

'Have you thought about staying a little bit longer, Dr Thorne?' Eunice asked. 'Six months isn't very long and David Cutler really needs to hang up his stethoscope. You staying on to help Matt would be the perfect solution all round.'

'Um…I hadn't really thought about staying much longer

than the allotted time,' Kellie said, carefully avoiding Matt's eyes. 'I've put in an application for a posting at Byron Bay. I could have gone back to my old job in Newcastle but my family need more time to get used to being on their own.'

'Oh, well, it's early days yet,' Eunice said, and made her way back out to the kitchen.

Matt looked at Kellie. 'Is it true?' he asked. 'Are you applying for a placement at Byron Bay once your time here is up?'

Kellie picked up her water glass and examined the ice cubes rather than meet his eyes. 'I have a few options I'm exploring at present,' she said. 'I don't recall making any promises about staying longer than the six months.'

Matt swallowed. 'No...I guess you didn't.' He waited before adding, 'I have some business to see to in Brisbane. I'll be away for a couple of weeks at the most. Will you be all right on your own? David Cutler said he'd do what he can to help.'

'Of course,' she said. 'I'll be fine.'

'Good...' he said, looking away again. 'That's good.'

'Matt, you seem a little on edge,' she said, after another beat or two of painful silence. 'I know things have been pretty strained between us since...well, since that night we...I mean I...you know, overstepped the mark, but it seems to be getting worse. Have I done something wrong? I mean, apart from that...that other thing...'

He pushed away his wineglass and met her gaze once more. 'No,' he said, twisting his mouth so that it almost smiled. 'It's not you. It's me.'

Kellie stopped breathing as she looked into those midnight-blue eyes. Her heart gave an irregular thump and her stomach felt hollow in spite of the generous helping of roast beef with all the trimmings she had not long ago consumed.

'I have something I need to do,' he went on. 'I should have done it well before now, but I guess I just wasn't quite ready.'

What? Kellie was about to ask when Eunice suddenly came in with a tray loaded with a dish of steaming apple crumble and custard, setting it down before them with a cheerful smile as Bob followed with the jug of cream.

'This is Matt's favourite dessert, isn't it, Matt?' Eunice said, dishing him out a huge helping.

'Not too much cream for me, thanks, Bob,' Matt said as his manager began to tilt the jug over his plate.

'What about you, Dr Thorne?' Bob asked, with the jug poised. 'Are you worried about your heart, like Matt, or do you like to indulge now and again?'

Kellie gave a strained smile. 'I guess a little bit of what you fancy is OK now and again, right?'

Two and a half weeks later Kellie sat on the back steps of the veranda and watched as the dog she had called Sylvie came up to take a treat out of her hand. 'There you go, sweetie,' she said encouragingly. 'That wasn't so hard now, was it?'

It was one of the most satisfying experiences Kellie had had in the time she had spent so far in Culwulla Creek, that and seeing the young mothers' group go from strength to strength.

Julie's boys had even settled down a bit. Ty had decided to go back to school so he could finish his leaver's certificate in order to become a mechanic which had pleased his mother no end.

Ruth had pulled herself back into the swing of things and for the last few days had been madly helping Trish prepare one of the pastoral property's biggest barns for the bachelors' and spinsters' ball, which was being held that evening.

Kellie was in two minds about whether to go or not. She

didn't fancy dancing and flirting playfully with the locals when the only man she wanted to be there wasn't planning to attend. She had heard via Trish that Matt's father had suddenly become ill, and instead of returning to Culwulla Creek as planned Matt had had to travel down to Sydney. Trish didn't seem to have any idea of when he was planning on getting back.

Kellie was all dressed up and ready to go to the ball when she heard the sound of a car pull up outside. She pushed the curtain aside and felt her stomach drop like an out-of-control lift when she saw Matt's tall figure unfold from his car.

She gave her wrists and neck another quick spray of perfume. Drawing in a shaky breath, she made her way to the front door, each step she took making her stomach perform another star jump.

He was stroking Sylvie under the chin when Kellie opened the door. He straightened and gave her a smile. 'Hi.'

'Hi.'

He shifted his weight from one foot to the other. 'You look nice,' he said. 'Great, in fact. You look great. Fabulous…' He cleared his throat. 'Really great.'

'Thank you.'

There was a little silence.

'I see you've tamed the dog,' he said, shifting his weight again.

'Yes, I've called her Sylvie.'

He cleared his throat once more. 'Er…that's a nice name.'

'Yes, it means from the forest,' Kellie said. 'I kind of thought it was appropriate. She sort of came from the bush, which is almost the same thing as a forest, right?'

He nodded and smiled. 'Er…right.'

'So…' She rolled her lips together. 'Are you going to the ball? I'm just about to leave so…' She left the sentence hanging.

'Are you sure you still qualify?' he asked.

She gave him a quizzical look. 'Qualify? What do you mean by qualify?'

He gave a little shrug and reached down again to stroke Sylvie, who was practically sitting on his left foot by now, gazing up at him adoringly. 'It's a bachelors' and spinsters' ball,' he said. 'Only single, unattached people are supposed to go.'

Kellie felt her heart join in with her stomach's complicated gymnastics routine. 'Um…last time I looked I was still single and unattached,' she said, trying to read his exasperatingly inscrutable expression.

His dark blue eyes locked on hers. 'Listen, Kellie, there's no point in me beating about the bush…' He suddenly smiled and corrected himself. 'Or the forest, as the case may be. The thing is I love you.'

She blinked at him. 'You…you do?'

'I do.'

'Wow…' she breathed.

His smile widened. 'Is that all you can say?'

'Oh, wow…' She looked up at him dreamily.

'I want you to marry me,' he said. 'I want you to be my wife.'

'But what about—'

He pressed the pad of his finger against her lips to stop her saying the name out loud. 'She's gone, Kellie. You were right, it was well and truly time to let her go. The thing is, I had done so ages ago but I hadn't really realised it until you came along. That's one of the reasons I went to Brisbane. I took her ashes and her photograph back to her parents and told them I was moving on with my life. I told them I was coming back here to ask you to be my wife. Will you do me the honour of being my partner in life, no matter where it leads us or whatever it throws at us?'

'Oh, wow… Oh, wow…'

Matt grinned at her. 'Is that a "yes" or a "maybe" or an "I'm still thinking about it"?'

Kellie could barely speak for joy. 'You really mean it? You *really* love me?'

He looked down at her tenderly. 'I've been trying to tell you for the last three weeks but every time I worked up the courage, someone would interrupt us,' he said.

'But I thought you were still in love with Madeleine?'

He gave a sigh and held her close. 'After Madeleine was killed, I grieved and heavily. I didn't see the point in having a life when she had been robbed of hers. But the truth is, she wasn't the love of my life. I think that's why I stayed away from another relationship for so long for then I would have to face up to the realisation I hadn't loved her the way she deserved to be loved.'

'Oh, Matt…'

He smiled down at her. 'I guess that's why you got under my skin from day one,' he said. 'You came bouncing into town with your propensity to mother and organise everyone, and I realised how I had never felt that sort of attraction before. It was like being hit right between the eyes.'

'Oh, Matt,' Kellie said again, hugging him tightly. 'I thought you didn't even notice me that first day on the plane.'

He lowered his chin to the top of her head, pulling her closer. 'I would have noticed you from the first second, but the truth was I was struggling with the aftermath of that trip to Brisbane for Madeleine's birthday. I had gone there intending to tell her parents I was ready to reclaim my life, but when I got there, I just couldn't seem to do it. They were so glad to see me, so pathetically grateful, that I felt a heel the whole time I was there.

'You were right when you said that deep down I was angry at Madeleine for dying. It shocked me to hear it but later when I thought about it I realised it was true. Anger is grief's second cousin, depression is its first. I was getting a little too close to both of them until you came along.'

Kellie looked up at him devotedly. 'I think I fell in love with you within the first day or two of meeting you. I didn't want to but I just couldn't help it. But I was so worried you would never be able to move on enough to love me back.'

He tucked a strand of her hair behind her ear with a touch so gentle she felt tears come to her eyes. 'I can't promise you in the months and years to come I won't sometimes think of Madeleine,' he said. 'I know it's not quite the same thing, but it's like asking you to never think of your mother. It's just not possible to forget the people who have touched you in some way during the course of your life. But I can promise you I will love you with my whole heart for the rest of our days. I don't care where we live, be it bush or beach, as long as you're with me I'll be the happiest man on earth.'

Kellie wrapped her arms around him, her smile as wide as it was radiant. 'I didn't really apply for that job at Byron Bay,' she confessed sheepishly. 'So, if it's all right, can I stay here with you?'

Matt grinned as he swept her up in his arms. 'You can stay with me as long as you like, starting from now,' he said, and carried her inside.